Russell A. Pitts is a former naval officer, teacher, professor, actor, and Buddhist monk. He is also a father and grandfather. Currently, he owns and operates a bed and breakfast in Upstate New York. *The Clonfert House Chronicles* is his first young adult fantasy series. *Part One: The Enchanters* was published in April 2020.

To Logan, Jarrad, Lilian, Sophia, Kaitlyn, Kendall, Bennett, Trae, Kiernan, Regan, Ayla, Gwenna, and Colin.

Russell A. Pitts

THE CLONFERT HOUSE CHRONICLES PART 2

Affey and the Green Maiden

AUSTIN MACAULEY PUBLISHERS™

LONDON • CAMBRIDGE • NEW YORK • SHARJAH

Ordering Information
Quantity sales: Special discounts are available on quantity purchases by corporations, associations, and others. For details, contact the publisher at the address below.

Publisher's Cataloging-in-Publication data
Pitts, Russell A.
The Clonfert House Chronicles Part 2

ISBN 9781638293804 (Paperback)
ISBN 9781638293811 (Hardback)
ISBN 9781638293828 (ePub e-book)

Library of Congress Control Number: 2022919164

www.austinmacauley.com/us

First Published 2022
Austin Macauley Publishers LLC
40 Wall Street, 33rd Floor, Suite 3302
New York, NY 10005
USA

mail-usa@austinmacauley.com
+1 (646) 5125767

To Jill Eggers, who has been a sounding board and good friend, and who was first to describe the *Clonfert House Chronicles* as 'spiritual fantasy'.

Prelude

The Far, Far, Distant Past
Mount Annapurna, Central Tibet
Winter

The Shaman, Jangchup Dawa, of the Bon Village at the foot of Mount Annapurna, was halfway up the treacherous path up the mountain when, without warning, a severe storm blew in over the mountain top. The snow whipped fiercely around him. The rapid snowfall and dropping temperature would only make his pilgrimage up the mountain to the Goddess Khandiravani's temple all the more hazardous. His bones rattled from the cold. His feet were almost frost bitten. The path to Khandiravani's temple was so steep and narrow that, should the Shaman slip and fall, he would plummet over the edge never to be seen again. He cried out for help to Khandiravani, the Goddess of his devotion.

> *"Khandiravani, I am your devoted disciple, Janchup Dawa, the Bon Shaman*
> *You are the Goddess who protects pilgrims like me.*
> *It is you who removes all obstacles from their way,*
> *Have pity on me.*
> *Rescue me.*
> *Without your aid I will surely perish here, on your mountain."*

The Shaman fought with each step to trudge up the mountain path, but the howling wind and blinding snow forced him back each time he tried to advance. He had been on the mountain path for six days and was only halfway to the temple. Every Shaman from the Bon village was required to make the journey to Khandiravani's temple every five years. Once they reached the temple they remained there for a month in study, prayer, and meditation. This was Jangchup Dawa's fifth pilgrimage. His previous pilgrimages, all made during the summer, were uneventful. He typically reached the temple three days after departing from his hermitage at the base of Mount Annapurna. He had never faced weather like this, though he knew two other shaman who attempted a winter ascent and perished. Would this pilgrimage be his last?

Jangchup Dawa, tried to take one more step up the steep grade of the path when he lost his footing and fell. Fortunately, he fell forward on his face and not sideways which would have seen him cast over the edge into the abyss below. He attempted to get up, but the snow was falling so hard that within minutes he was buried in it. He managed to keep his head just above the accumulating snow so that he could breathe. He said aloud in the howling wind, "I must get up and keep moving. If I stay here, the snow will suffocate me under a white drift on the mountain side. No one will find me until the spring thaw." The fierce wind carried his words up the mountain to Khandiravani's temple. He prayed to her one last time.

"My Goddess, Khandiravani,
You see my plight.
I am about to die here on your mountain.
I pray that you will invite me to be with you in my next life.
I do not want to die like this, choking on the snow,
But I accept my fate.
Remember me, a lowly shaman,
Who sought with all my heart,
To serve you.
To honor you."

Jangchup Dawa heard a tremendous roar above him. An avalanche. It raced down the mountain directly toward him. The avalanche was upon him in an instant. The snow began to fill the shaman's mouth imprisoning the scream he tried to let loose. He began to lose consciousness. The white that was about to bury him alive suddenly turned black. He announced to the snow around him, "I am dead." They were the last words he said before he passed out.

The avalanche continued to menace the path up Mount Annapurna to Khandiravani's Temple. Despite the power of the avalanche, the shaman's prayer reached Khandiravani. She swept down from her temple on the top of the mountain and pulled the shaman from near death. She whisked him up to the safety and warmth of her temple. There, the shaman recovered over the course of several days. When he regained consciousness, the Goddess Khandiravani was sitting there with him.

"Jangchup Dawa, I see you are recovering."

The Shaman could not believe his eyes. There, at the foot of his straw cot, sat the Goddess Khandiravani. The shaman recalled what his guru taught him about the Goddess. He could almost hear his guru's voice. "No one ever actually sees the Goddess. She is all myth and legend. Khandiravani dwells in a realm reserved for the gods and goddesses. The closest anyone gets to seeing her is in the paintings on temple walls or the statues displayed everywhere in the villages. The stories about Khandiravani tell of her intercession on the behalf of her followers, but those stories are from a time long, long ago." Yet, despite what the shaman's guru said, here she was, sitting a chair at the foot of Jangchup Dawa's straw cot talking to him.

"I see you were not expecting me, shaman," she said warmly.

The shaman wanted to get out of his bed and prostrate out of respect before her, but his legs failed him.

"Goddess, forgive me, I cannot move my legs to get out of this bed and pay my proper respects to you."

Khandiravani smiled which put the shaman at ease. "My dear shaman, your whole life has been one of duty to me. As for your legs, give them another day and they will work fine. You know you almost died on the path?"

"Goddess, I surely would have perished if you had not rescued me. I am not worthy of your intercession."

The Goddess Khandiravani got up from the chair and sat on the edge of the shaman's straw cot. "I heard your prayer. It was carried up to me by the Wind Horse God. I would not leave you there alone on my mountain to die. A shaman such as yourself is needed in my world. There is more for you to do before you die." The Goddess knew exactly what was in store for the shaman.

"Khandiravani, all I ask is that I may live long enough to repay you for your kindness," the Shaman said humbly.

Khandiravani took the shaman's hand in hers and told him, "You will live longer than that. You arrived just in time. I need a shaman."

"You need a shaman?" Jangchup Dawa was stunned by the Goddess's words. The Goddess was more powerful than any shaman. For what possible reason could she need a shaman?

"I do, Jangchup Dawa, choose you as my shaman." Khandiravani got up from the straw cot to leave, but before she did, she turned to the shaman.

"I will return tomorrow. Then we will discuss what is next for you. Until then, let my attendants nurse you back to health. There is another journey you must yet take. It begins in two days." Khandiravani disappeared.

No sooner had she left than one of her attendants arrived with potions, ointments, tea, and a most delicious biscuit. The shaman ate heartily then fell into a hard asleep. He woke up the next morning to a bright sun shining into his room.

"You are awake. Wonderful." The Goddess Khandiravani was sitting in a chair in the corner of the room illuminated by the rays of the sun. The shaman thought it was the most natural thing for the sun to do. Yesterday, the shaman was so exhausted when he first met the Goddess that he didn't pay any attention to her appearance. But, illuminated by the morning sun, she was a wonder. Her blue-black hair shimmered in the sunbeams. Her head was adorned with a golden crown topped with many small figures. The Shaman did not know who or what the figures were. Her gown was as white as the snow on the mountain. He skin was a soft, buttery gold. Her eyes were as blue as the vast sky. There was no statue of her anywhere that was a glorious as she was at this moment sitting in the chair drenched in morning sunlight. Her beauty took his breath away.

Khandiravani asked the shaman, "have you tried to walk yet? Time is passing. There are things that must be attended to." As she finished her sentence, she crossed from the chair to stand next to the shaman's straw cot.

"Not yet, Goddess," the shaman said as he started to get out of bed. Khandiravani held out her hand to help him. The shaman hesitated before taking it. Was it proper to touch the hand of a Goddess? He took her hand in his anyway.

"There," she said. "You can walk."

The shaman was quite surprised that he could walk without any pain or difficulty since he was so crippled just yesterday. *It was yesterday, wasn't it?* he thought. It was as if he had not been injured at all. Whatever Khandiravani's guardians gave him was miraculous.

"Thank you, Goddess. I am indebted to you forever." The shaman walked around the room excited to have recovered so well and so soon.

"Now, to our business, Shaman." Khandiravani indicted the shaman should follow her.

The Goddess Khandiravani led the shamanto room adjacent to the one where he recovered. He was led into Khandiravani's meditation room. A golden altar was against the wall. The only things adorning the altar were two butter lamps that were already lit. Several cushions were arranged on the floor around the altar. Incense rose from three cauldrons. There was one cushion that was on a raised platform. Khandiravani sat there. She pointed to the one on the floor directly in front of her. The shaman sat down there. While the Shaman arranged himself on the cushion, Khandiravani closed her eyes and quietly recited some prayers. Once the shaman was settled on his cushion, the Goddess asked him a question. It was a question the shaman never asked himself even though he devoted his life to her.

"Shaman, you have devoted your whole life me. Tell me, what do you know of me?"

The shaman was both surprised and proud of how quickly an answer came to him. It was short, simple, and direct. It was as if the answer had been waiting to fall out of his mouth.

"I know that you dwell here, on Mount Annapurna. You are the White Goddess because of your command over the winter elements on this mountain. You are a protector, a guide. You have a reputation for being fierce, though kind. The thing you are most revered for is your power to face down any malignant spirit."

Khandiravani didn't say anything for a while. She sat motionless on her raised platform. The Shaman fidgeted on his cushion unsure what to do or say. At last, she spoke to him.

"All you said is true. What I am going to tell you next you may not understand right away. Yet, in time, you will know that where I am taking you is your destiny. You will be happier there with me and the others than you have ever been." She waited for the Shaman to consider what she said.

Jangchup Dawa, the shaman from the Bon village, was dazzled by her words. Especially since they came so suddenly after his rescue and recovery. Not just every shaman, but every person he knew wanted to be as happy as possible. It was what he longed for. It was what he helped other people attain. Yet, there was something she said that kept repeating in his mind, "…Where I am taking you…with me…the others." *Were they going somewhere together? Who were these 'others'?*

"I can see that you want to know if we are going somewhere together," the Goddess observed.

"Yes, I am, Goddess. I came here as a simple pilgrim to fulfill my duties as a shaman. Your words to me…I don't know what to say. What are you trying to tell me Goddess?"

"For now, I must be brief, Shaman. Once we have arrived where we are going you will understand what is expected of you. You and I are leaving here tomorrow. Forever. Neither you nor I will ever return here. There is a spirit realm that needs a protector. My sisters have decided I am the one to go there."

"Sisters? You have sisters?" Nowhere in his studies had there been any mention of the Goddess's sisters.

"Yes, Shaman, I have sisters, six, in fact. We are not sisters in the human sense. We are spirit sisters. Something else you will one day come to understand." She explained further. "Each of us sisters have a particular influence in the worlds of spirits and in your realm, the human realm. Each of us is associated with a color the symbolizes our individual gifts. My Blue Sister is a bringer of happiness and joy. My Orange Sister is a liberator from negative thoughts and emotions. My Yellow Sister ensures fertility, abundance, and prosperity. My Black Sister is an avenger. Of course, I am the White Sister because I dwell here in the snow and because I am the bringer of peace. I am the youngest sister."

Jangchup Dawa was getting more and more confused. He asked Khandiravani, "so, you are bringing peace somewhere and you need me to help you?"

"Not exactly, though peace is always my concern," Khandiravani said. "As I mentioned, Shaman, I will be brief. I have much to do today. We are leaving in the morning at sunrise."

Despite his confusion, the shaman had a feeling that something extraordinary was about to happen to him.

"You mentioned others, Goddess. Who are they?"

"I will tell you in a minute. First, tonight is a night that will change everything for you. Tonight, you must undergo a transformation. Where we are going together, mandates you abandon that part of you that is human. What is required is that you become fully your spirit self. You cannot enter this realm

16

unless you do. I will make this manifest in you tonight while you sleep. There is nothing for you to do except to accept your destiny. When you awake in the morning, you will be fully spirit. Memories of your human self will remain, but, over time, they will fade away, such will be your happiness in your new life. You will also have a new name. It will be a name that signals to all the creatures in this new realm that you are one of them. I hope this does not frighten you."

"Not at all Goddess. My life has been one of yearning for my spirit self. And you, Goddess. What is expected of you in this place where we are going?"

"As of tomorrow, I will become the Green Sister. It is necessary for this new realm to have a sister who is aligned with the wind and the woods. In this new realm we will abide in a sacred tree. You asked about the others I mentioned. You and I will be joined by six others who will be just like you. You and they will serve as my guardians and protectors."

The shaman asked, "What will happen here. Where are these others coming from?"

"A new White Sister will arrive shortly after we depart. My sisters have made the arrangements for the others who will join us. These other guardians will arrive a few days after us. We are going ahead to prepare for them. Now, you must excuse me. I have much to do before tomorrow morning. Please enjoy the rest of your day. My attendants will visit you at sunset to administer a potion. It will initiate your transformation. You will fall into a mystic dream. I won't see you again until you wake tomorrow morning. I will be there when you awaken. Do you have any questions before I go?"

"I do, Goddess. It might be silly one. You said that when I wake tomorrow, I will have a new name. Can you tell me what it will be?"

Khandiravani chuckled. "It will be a fine spirit name. One that will fit nicely in our new realm. You will be called Botsam, my chief guardian."

The shaman, Jangchup Dawa, laughed heartily at his new, very odd spirit name. "And you Goddess. How shall I address you when I am Botsam?"

"When you awake tomorrow morning, you will know me as The Green Maiden." She left to make her final preparations to leave.

The shaman took the Goddess's advice. The sun would not set for another few hours, so he took the time to wander through the Goddess's temple complex. He knew it would be the last time he would be able to do so.

Even though it was the middle of the winter season, the flower beds which stretched in all directions were blooming through the dusting of snow that covered them. They were as fragrant as they were in springtime. The shaman lingered in the garden just outside the building where he was recovering. He took in deep swallows of the crisp, perfumed air. He thought, *if only I could stay here forever*. The sun slipped behind a mountain to the west. Two of the Goddess's attendants appeared.

"It is time for you to retire to your chambers, Shaman." The two attendants spoke as if they had a single voice. The shaman Jangchup Dawa took one, last look over the temple grounds before he ducked through the entrance and followed the two attendants to his small room.

Laid out on his straw cot was a muslin night shirt. The attendants stepped outside the room so he could change into it. Once he was finished, they re-entered. One of them had a tray with what looked like tea. There was a bowl filled with sweets. She put it down on a table by the hearth. The other attendant carried a bundle wrapped in green velvet that was tied with a silver stand. She placed the bundle on the chair at the floor of the shaman's straw cot. The shaman stood in his muslin robe, barefoot, in the middle of the room. He waited for instructions.

The attendant who brough in the tray said, "when we leave you must eat as many of the sweets as you can. You don't need to eat them all, but please try. It is imperative that you drink all of this potion." She pointed to the teacup. "As soon as you finish the potion you must go to bed. You will sleep through your transformation."

The shaman kept didn't have anything to say.

"When you wake in the morning, you will dress in the clothes that are in this bundle," the other attendant said pointing to the velvet wrapped parcel on the chair.

"I understand," the shaman said. "What will you do with my shaman robes? They are sacred to me."

"You will have no need of them any longer. Out of respect for your vows, the Goddess has given instructions that they are to be handed down to a shaman in need. She hopes that is what you want."

"Since you have said I won't need them any longer, then yes. Please make sure they go to someone who needs them. A shaman in my own village would be nice."

"We will see to it," they said in that one voice they shared. "Goodnight, Shaman." They left.

The shaman Jangchup Dawa carried the tray over to his straw cot. He sat with it on his lap and ate all the sweets in the bowl. He couldn't resist. When he finished the last bite, he gulped down the cup of potion, placed it back on the tray, returned the tray to the floor by the hearth. He wanted to unwrap the velvet parcel to examine his new clothes, but he felt suddenly very drowsy. He made it to his cot just in time. He fell onto the bed and slipped into a deep sleep.

The shaman was awakened the next morning when bright sunlight streamed through the window in his small room. One of the two attendants had flung open the curtain. The other attendant was busy unwrapping the green velvet parcel.

"Time to get up." For the first time, the attendant did not address him as 'shaman'.

The shaman rubbed the sleep from his eyes. He swung his legs over the edge of the cot so he could stand up. Something wasn't right. His feet didn't reach the floor as they should. The two attendants were watching him carefully. He had to jump a little to get off the bed.

"Am I shorter," he asked the attendants.

"Yes, you are. You might want to put these clothes on," she said as she laid them out on his straw cot. "The Goddess is on her way. You need to be dressed by the time she gets here. Please, hurry. There is a bowl of water with a set of towels and brushes for you to groom yourself. Please don't waste your time." With that the two attendants departed.

The shaman noticed that all his old clothes were gone. He quickly washed his face, brushed his teeth, and looked in the small mirror they brought him. The face reflecting back at him was not his, at least not in every detail. He could tell it was him, but he was smaller. His hair, once long and flowing, was cropped short. He no longer had a beard. All in all, the shaman liked what he saw. He was younger than when he went to sleep.

"So," he said to his reflection, "this is Botsam."

He quickly put on the clothes that had been laid out for him on the straw cot. White under garments that were soft and warm. Pale yellow stockings that came up over his knees. He had never worn socks before. He only wore reed sandals. There was a lacy, honey colored shirt. A suit of matching emerald green velvet trousers that came just to his knees and a doublet. They all fit him perfectly. He was as comfortable in them as he had been in his tattered shaman's robes. A pair of dark brown leather boots sat on the floor waiting for him to step into them. This would the first time the shaman had ever worn shoes. He worried he would not like the feel of them. When he put them on, he could tell his feet were inside them. Yet, they were so soft and supple that he might as well have been barefoot. As he walked around his chamber bouncing up and down on his toes the Goddess arrived. She too had changed.

The Goddess Khandiravani was not who stood in the shaman's chamber. Standing in front of him was a creature of rare beauty. She was taller than the Goddess. Her skin was emerald green, almost the same shade as the shaman's new clothes. Her eyes were a deep gold. Her hair was auburn streaked with a gold that matched her eyes. She was surrounded by a pale green glow. On seeing her, the shaman dropped into a prostration at her feet.

"Come now, Botsam," she said. "We will have none of that." She reached down to help him get up off the floor.

He stood in front of her looking up into her gentle, smiling face. "You look…I don't know what to say, Goddess."

"We will have no more talk of Goddess either. You may call me 'mistress' or 'Green Maiden'."

"Yes, mistress, I mean Green Maiden. Oh, I will get it sooner or later."

"I am sure that you will, Botsam." She emphasized his name. He liked the way it sounded coming from the Green Maiden.

"It's time to go." The Green Maiden didn't give Botsam a chance to reply. She swung her emerald robes around him. Uttering an incantation, she whisked them away on the wind to the Eo Mugna Tree.

Time: The Present

Chapter 1
The Eo Mugna Tree Affey's Secret

Affey had a secret, though it would remain hidden even from her until the Green Maiden revealed it. When Affey was rescued from the Western Quarter's assault on Clonfert House and brought to the Eo Mugna Tree for safety, the Green Maiden had her first inkling that Affey was different than other mortals. At this first encounter with Affey, the Green Maiden experienced a profound, inexplicable sense that Affey was meant to replace her. This feeling disturbed the Green Maiden. How could a human girl possibly replace her? Only fay had ever become Green Maiden. Could it be possible? She had to consult the Annals of The Sisterhood that were entrusted to each Green Maiden. The Annals of the Sisterhood laid out, in detail, the entire lineage of the Green Maidens back thirty-five hundred years. The Green Maiden had not referred to the Annals of The Sisterhood since she first became the seventh Green Maiden four hundred ninety-nine years ago. Had she missed some detail, some moment in time when a Green Maiden was a mortal and not fay? Was she wrong about Affey? The Annals must have an answer.

The Annals of The Sisterhood explain that every five hundred years a new Green Maiden appears. The current Green Maiden was the seventh in the lineage. Affey, she was sure, was to be the eighth, but how? Why? The Green Maiden confirmed that nowhere in the Annals of The Sisterhood was there a mention of a human becoming the Green Maiden. Green Maidens were always from the spirit realm. The first Green Maiden had been a Goddess, another a sprite, two were nymphs, two fairies, and she, the seventh was born a will-o-the-wisp. She re-read the section that described the birth of the Green Maidens looking for any hint that would explain Affey's appearance at this time in the history of the Sisterhood.

First, the Green Maiden re-read the general statement describing how a new Green Maiden is born. She read that, for all spirits, not just Green Maidens, their birth is linked to the birth of a human child. When the human child lets out its first cry, the infant fairy who is joined to them is born. But, in the case of the Green Maiden, the human birth is both more unusual and extraordinary. The spirit infant must be a female. Males are utterly forbidden. The human child must be born with green eyes and golden hair. Her skin color makes no difference. In fact, several Green Maidens have had human birth partners that were Asian, African, Indian. The spirit infants color of hair, eyes, skin is unimportant. She would transform into her emerald essence when the time was right. The human infants walked earlier than most. They could speak in simple words shortly after their birth. The spirit infant was different. The spirit infant who would become the Green Maiden spoke in complete, sophisticated sentences within moments of their birth. They sprouted their wings within days rather than years as is typical for a spirit. The infant spirit would eventually be confirmed as the new Green Maiden by passing a test known as 'The Ritual of the Seven Pomegranate Seeds' administered by a spirit midwife who had been trained to perform this most sacred ritual.

The Green Maiden decided to read through the birth and discovery records of every Green Maiden. The account of her own birth and discovery as the seventh Green Maiden read as follows:

THE SEVENTH GREEN MAIDEN
Five days ago, the seventh Green Maiden was born. All the heavenly and earthly signs so indicated. They described a golden haired, green eyed human child was born in Wales. The signs also augured that the spirit infant joined to this human child was likewise born at the same time, also in Wales. Most unusual for both to be born so close to each other. The Midwife, Rhianwen, was immediately dispatched to scour the tree tops throughout the Welsh forests for a new born fairy infant. After three days she found a beautiful, green eyed, golden haired will-o-the-wisp infant in a nest atop an ancient oak in Cloedf-y-Celyn, the Fairy Glen. When she found this spirit child, she was fast asleep in the arms of her mother. Her mother was fearful that the midwife had come to steal her baby. Once Rhianwen explained why she had come, the mother was at first over-joyed at what this meant. Then she was sad knowing that the day would come

when her daughter would be taken away to begin her transformation into the Green Maiden. She placed the child in Rhianwen's arms. Rhianwen performed 'The Ritual of the Seven Pomegranate Seeds'. Rhianwen placed one pomegranate seed on the infant fairy's forehead, one on her throat, one on her heart, and held the other four in the palm of her closed left hand, all as required by the ritual. No sooner had she finished placing the pomegranate seeds than the child woke up from her slumber. Looking up at Rhianwen's gentle face, the infant spirit smiled. She reached out for Rhianwen's left hand that held the four pomegranate seeds. She opened Rhianwen's fingers and removed just one seed. She offered this single pomegranate seed to her mother. Her mother wept knowing that this simple gesture confirmed that her daughter was the new Green Maiden. Rhianwen explained that she would visit every month until the child could survive on her own. This should take about 15 years or so. Rhianwen departed. Entered this 19th day of October 1520

The Green Maiden recalled that the next fifteen years of her life passed quickly. The day Rhianwen came to bring her home to the Eo Mugna Tree, she was accompanied by the dying, sixth Green Maiden, whom she would replace. Yet, the sixth Green Maiden charmed her mother into forgetting her so she would not feel sad. Once the charm had set, the sixth Green Maiden, Rhianwen, and she flew back to the Eo Mugna Tree. There, she learned what was expected of her as the seventh Green Maiden. She mastered the skills that only a Green Maiden could possess. She was transformed just before the sixth Green Maiden perished. It was all in accord with the unbroken lineage of the Green Maidens. Now, it was her turn to teach and transform Affey, the eighth Green Maiden. Of this she was certain. Yet, she could not find in her re-reading of the Annals of The Sisterhood any record of a human child becoming a Green Maiden. Perhaps more importantly, there was no mention of any mortal birth that should have been already recorded in the Annals if Affey was her successor. In fact, there was no mention whatsoever of any birth regarding her replacement. Why was there no mention, at all, of the eighth Green Maiden in the Annals? The Annals were silent on the matter. Did this mean the lineage of the Green Maiden was ending? What was she to do? There was also one other development that worried her.

It was clear to her that, having lived 499 years, that this year would be her last. The exact timing of her passing was not fixed. She only knew it would be sometime this year.

When she first rescued Affey during the confrontation with Adena at Clonfert House, the Green Maiden knew, she just knew, that Affey was to be the eighth Green Maiden. Yet, she couldn't fathom why a mortal would replace her. How was she to transform this human girl into the Green Maiden? There was no precedent for such an event. Green Maidens are alone in the world, except for her seven guardians. How could a human girl, whose kind depend on so many human relationships, possibly thrive under these circumstances? How could the human body, mind, and soul survive for five hundred years? Only the strongest among the mortals lived to be a hundred years old. There was no one she could turn to for advice. Could the Oracle of the Dar Lantern be of help? She would have to think about going to see the Oracle. For now, though, the Green Maiden would have to rely on her instincts to transform Affey from a human teenager into the eighth Green Maiden. Her own green essence was fading. There was no time to lose. She decided then and there that, despite her misgivings and the absence of any reference in the Annals of the Sisterhood, Affey was to become the eighth Green Maiden.

Her first task was to reveal to Affey what was in store for her, not just now, but for centuries into the future. Affey was brought to the Eo Mugna Tree to be the Green Maiden's protégé, a sort of special helper. At that time, it was true. Now, however, The Green Maiden had to tell Affey that she was to replace her – for five hundred years! She had to wait for just the right moment.

The Green Maiden also had to confront her own mortality. When she was called upon to assist Clonfert House in the defeat of Adena and her cohorts from the Western Quarter, the Green Maiden noticed that her powers were not as strong as they once were. Whenever she had to deploy one of them, she would suffer from crippling exhaustion afterward. When she had to bind Uncle Rabbit and the generals to the roots of the Eo Mugna Tree, she had to go to her bed chamber and sleep for a day. When she bound the Mistress Pyx, a human, beneath the Tree, she suffered from a confusing pain. She never determined what that pain was. These were all signs that her time as Green Maiden was on the wane. Her hair was thinning. Some of its golden luster was fading. Sometimes, her eyes failed her. It took her just a second or two longer to vanish into the air. Her time was coming to an end. The Green Maiden knew it was time to put things in order so that Affey's transition into her new life as the eighth Green Maiden would be complete before she has to pass on to the next realm. Little did the Green Maiden know that Affey's transformation had to be accomplished more quickly than she anticipated. Events were unfolding that required it.

Chapter 2
The Eo Mugna Tree
Affey's Secret Revealed

Since arriving at the Eo Mugna Tree, Affey sensed something awakening in her. Her experience leading to the defeat of Adena at Clonfert House matured her beyond her years. It instilled a confidence in her that she didn't know she had. Whatever this new awakening was, it felt powerful. What kind of power she couldn't fathom? She liked the way it rippled through her sometimes. At no time did she fear it or doubt it. She just wondered what it was and why it was happening. Whatever this new power was, it made her experience during the defeat of Adena seem superficial and weak.

Not long after this feeling began, Affey realized, quite to her surprise, that she no longer felt the need to go home or visit Clonfert House. She still wanted to see her twin sister, Minda, but that feeling too was diminished. Each passing day with the Green Maiden, Affey felt more and more that she was home. Of course, she had to remind herself that her time here with the Green Maiden was temporary. She was here to learn what she could, but eventually she would return to Clonfert House. There were moments when she wasn't so sure. Did it have something to do with the power she felt rising in her? The more frequently she felt it, the more she was convinced that it was some sort of spirit awakening. Not a spiritual awakening, but the waking up of a spirit nature in her. She was thrilled with it at times. Other times, she didn't know what to make of it. It was all very confusing. There were fleeting moments when all Affey wanted was to be with her twin sister, Minda, back at Clonfert House. Whenever she had those thoughts, they faded quickly. Leaving the Eo Mugna Tree and the Green Maiden was unthinkable. She had to ask the Green Maiden about it all. Affey decided to talk with the Green Maiden about her feelings the next morning during breakfast.

Affey set down her cup of tea, patted her lips with her napkin, then asked. "Mistress, I have been here for several weeks. You have shown me the nearby forests and glens. Your seven guardians have been most welcoming, especially Botsam. I am growing quite fond of him. I spend my days immersed in the beauty of this forest. Your lair, that you so generously share with me, is extraordinarily elegant. The food here is delicious. I have books to read at my leisure. Nothing seems to be required of me. Yet, I feel there is more I should be doing." Affey hesitated to tell the Green Maiden that she felt something was happening to her, something she didn't understand.

The Green Maiden stopped eating, placed her knife and fork across her plate and said, "my dear, dear Affey. You must be patient. You have much so very much to learn. Living in the spirit realm is different than the human realm. It takes time to adjust. Just enjoy yourself. Take the time to become familiar with what it is like being here in this realm," She didn't say a thing about becoming a Green Maiden. The time wasn't right.

"I expected things would be different somehow, but to be honest with you, Mistress, there is this feeling growing in me. It started when I was last here. This feeling is powerful somehow. There are days when it is exciting, but then there are days when it frightens me. Can you help me understand what it is?"

The Green Maiden knew that Affey would eventually ask about what was happening to her. The Green Maiden thought it would be at least another year, though, before Affey would ask. It was the same thing that happened to her, but it took the Green Maiden almost two years to ask the sixth Green Maiden the same question. The Green Maiden had forgotten that time passes differently in the spirit realm than in the human realm. Affey must learn to be patient or her transformation might be incomplete before the Green Maiden had to depart from this world.

Affey sense of the passing of time was still from the human experience of it. Affey learned from her classes at Saint Brendan's Academy that spirit time is not the same as human time. Supposedly, time passes in the spirit realm much slower. Her studies did not prepare her for the actual living in spirit time. When combined with the rising power in her, it was overwhelming.

The Green Maiden had to remind herself that, once Affey understood how time moves in the fairy realm, then Affey's transformation into the new Green Maiden would evolve as it should. She also reminded herself that if Affey couldn't make the adjustment, her transformation would fail, thus bringing an end to the lineage of the Green Maiden. That must not be allowed to happen.

The Green Maiden took Affey's question as an opportunity to plant the seed for Affey's transformation as the next Green Maiden, but the time was still not quite right to tell her everything.

"Affey, the first thing you must learn is that time passes differently here. Compared to the human realm, time passes here quite slowly. A minute, an hour, a day here is a mere second or two or three in the human realm. You must accept and understand this. Take me as an example. Let me ask you a question, Affey. How old do you think I am?"

Affey took her time to look more closely at the Green Maiden than she had ever done before. She noticed a few strands of grey in the Green Maiden's golden hair. Fine lines etched the corners of her eyes. Her green skin was not as emerald green as it once was. Her chin sagged. The corners of her lips crinkled. The Green Maiden seemed to radiate less of her energy. It never occurred to Affey that the Green Maiden was any age at all. Wasn't the Green Maiden eternal? Would the Green Maidens eventually die like everything else? As she looked at the Green Maiden and thought about her age, Affey was no longer sure. The Green Maiden was aging, that was obvious for sure, but just how old could she be? Considering that time in the spirit realm moved more slowly than the human realm, Affey asked herself, how to guess the age of a Green Maiden? Surely, I cannot think in human terms. Did the slower movement of time mean one aged faster or slower in this realm? Did the spirits even count years? Affey ventured a guess.

"A hundred years old?"

The Green Maiden laughed. "Oh, Affey, you have so much to learn." She didn't respond directly to Affey's guess.

Affey tried again. "One hundred and twenty? Surely you are not younger, are you?"

The Green Maiden took Affey by the hand and led her out onto the edge a large branch of the Eo Mugna Tree that overlooked the valley below. The Green Maiden decided this was the moment to reveal Affey's destiny. There would not be a better opportunity.

"Tell me what you see Affey," the Green Maiden said as they looked out over the valley.

Affey's first inclination was to describe the valley as she would have in human terms, but she hesitated. She saw the valley differently. Yes, she saw trees, meadows, the stream that meandered through the valley, the distant hills. That was what she expected to see. But the way she saw now was something beyond anything she had experienced before. Was she seeing with spirit eyes? Standing there, hand in hand with the Green Maiden, every leaf, every blade of grass, every stone and rock in the stream bed, every creature for as far as her vision took her was immediately present before her. There was a hum all around her. She could hear many different voices, some talking, others laughing, some singing. She heard them all at once, yet each distinct. All things were as a single moment, a single universe. What astonished Affey the most, was the sense that she was intimately intertwined with this universe and its creatures. She felt as though she was a part of every living thing. The restless, power awakening inside Affey swelled inside her. She thought, *this is the world as it really is. This is what has been happening to me. I am becoming one with this world.* She squeezed the Green Maiden's hand.

Together they looked out over the universe of worlds before them. The Green Maiden waved her left hand out in front of her. This signaled all the fairies, elves, sprites, gnomes, nymphs, brownies, knockers, every spirit who lived in the valley to appear. Hundreds and hundreds of them came out from their homes to look up at the Green Maiden and Affey. They were all shapes and sizes, myriad colors. Those that could, flew up to the branch where Affey and the Green Maiden stood. The air was filled with the buzzing of their wings. They talked and giggled among themselves. They were fascinated by Affey. When the last one arrived, they all stopped their chatter. They hovered in the air before the Green Maiden and Affey. Together with those spirits still on the ground, they bowed together to the Green Maiden. Then, they all also bowed to Affey. The Green Maiden bowed in return. With a flourish and a song, the fairies flew off back to their homes. Life in the valley below them returned to normal. The Green Maiden turned to see how Affey reacted.

"Why did the spirits bow to me?" Even though she asked, Affey suspected that knew the answer. Still, it was not easy for her to accept. Affey had not considered the far-reaching, long-lasting consequences of the answer. If she was right, Affey would be here with the Green Maiden for a very, very long time, even in human terms. There would be no going back to Clonfert House. No more living with her twin sister, Minda. She would never live at home again. Affey expected these realizations to be painful. To her surprise, it all seemed to be exactly as it should be. Why?

The Green Maiden let Affey's question about the spirits bowing to her hang in the air between them. It was time to reveal everything to Affey.

"Affey, this realm will one day be yours. You are more than my protégé. You are more than a special helper for me. You are my successor. You are to become the eighth Green Maiden."

The Green Maiden and Affey stood together for looking over the valley below them. They held each other's hands as though they too were one.

In that moment, standing hand-in-hand with the Green Maiden, Affey understood her fate. It was true, she would never again live at home or at Clonfert House again. Her twin sister would visit her. It would be a cruel realm if they could not see each other. The same would be true of Affey's parents, and Michael, and Kevin. However, it would be different from now on. She would forever be apart from them in many, many ways. It struck Affey that all that was happening to her, her becoming a Green Maiden, was because the Green Maiden holding her hand was going to die. Again, Affey accepted the fate of the Green Maiden. Someday it would be her fate too. As she looked up at the Green Maiden, Affey knew exactly, how old the Green Maiden was. She didn't know how she knew. She just did. Affey turned to the Green Maiden.

"I know how old you are, Mistress." Affey took both the Green Maiden's hands in her own.

"You are almost five hundred years old. Someday I will be too." Affey didn't explain how she knew, and the Green Maiden didn't ask. It was just as it should be.

The Green Maiden embraced Affey. They stood on the edge of the branch overlooking the valley until the sun nearly set.

"Affey," the Green Maiden began, "there is so very much that lay ahead for you, for both of us. Today was just the beginning. Let's go back up to our home in the branches and rest for the night."

The Green Maiden led them back to her lair in the highest branches of the Eo Mugna Tree. Affey slept restlessly. Her dreams were filled with images from her past and perhaps her future. She wasn't sure. Her twin sister, Minda, who was now a senior student at Clonfert House, appeared often. Affey missed her sister. When would she see her again? What did her dreams mean?

Once Affey was asleep the Green Maiden planned to go and visit the Oracle at the Cave of the Dar Lantern. She needed guidance on how to lead Affey through her transformation. Since there were no precedents for a human becoming the Green Maiden, maybe the Oracle would have some insights. Maybe the Oracle could shed light on the circumstances of Affey's birth which were not recorded in the Annals of The Sisterhood. Maybe that would help. Hopefully, the Oracle would have some advice for the Green Maiden on how to proceed. However, just as she was about to set out to visit the Oracle, an ancient sprite tumbled into the Eo Mugna Tree.

Chapter 3
The Eo Mugna Tree Terrible News

"Mistress? Mistress? Are you here?" A raspy, breathless old voice called out from a lower branch of the Eo Mugna tree.

The Green Maiden's Chief Guardian, Botsam, confronted the visitor. "Who calls on the Green Maiden at this hour? Don't you know it is rude to call upon my mistress without forewarning?"

"Sir, my name is Master Foote. I come from the Western Quarter, which, as you must know, is in chaos since the death of Adena and the disappearance of the three generals. Please, I must see the Green Maiden. It is urgent."

Botsam took the measure of the old sprite who clung to the branch gasping for breath. "She is here, but asleep. This must wait until the dawn. You are exhausted. Let us provide you a place to rest for the night." Botsam started to lead the old sprite to a guest room up in the branches.

"Please, sir, this cannot wait. I am more than exhausted. I am quite ill as are many of us in the Western Quarter. We need the Green Maiden's help."

Above them, the Green Maiden listened. She floated down to the branch where the old sprite stood clutching the branch where he landed.

"Master Foote." She addressed him formally because she knew him to be an honorable sprite.

"Yes, Mistress, it is I. We have met before, but it was many decades ago."

"I remember you, Master Foote. You were in Adena's court if I recall." She was a little suspicious of this old sprite, but would treat him with all kindness nonetheless since he was clearly distressed.

"I was at that time. For the past several years I have been left alone to my hobbies. However, recent events have bought me back from my cottage to help my kin. Please, hear what I have to say." He had difficulty breathing.

34

"Master Foote, you don't look well even for one as ancient as you." The Green Maiden was concerned. No species of spirit got as sick as he was. Something was terribly, terribly wrong.

"That is my reason for coming to you, Mistress. We have all fallen quite ill. We have been cursed by the Sorcerer Corradhu."

"Corradhu," the Green Maiden whispered the name with a combination of disdain and fear.

The Sorcerer Corradhu was the leader of the Stregheria. He dwelled with his witches and warlocks at the Su Nuraxi in Barumini, Sardinia. The Stregheria have occupied this nuraghe for over forty-five hundred years. Rarely did they venture off the island and then only to foray onto the Italian mainland. This was a disturbing development. Why had the Sorcerer Corradhu entered into the Western Quarter? What curse had he cast upon its fairies? Until the birth of Corradhu, the Stregheria were a peaceful coven. Though they could cast 'war curses' to defend themselves, in their entire history they never initiated an aggressive confrontation. That all changed under the Sorcerer Corradhu's leadership. It was known throughout the spirit realms that Corradhu and his coven had established sinister footholds in Naples, Bologna, Pisa, Venice, and Syracuse. What was he planning for the Western Quarter?

"Master Foote, tell me this. How long has the Sorcerer Corradhu been in the Western Quarter?"

"It has only been a matter of days, but he has caused much harm." Master Foote struggled to speak.

"Has help been sought from any other quarter," the Green Maiden asked.

"Yes, Mistress. A messenger was dispatched to Clonfert House to ask for help." Master Foote was growing very tired. He could barely stand. His journey to the Green Maiden was arduous for one as old as he was. What he didn't tell the Green Maiden was that he came of his own accord. No one in the Western Quarter thought to enlist the help of the Green Maiden. When he raised the possibility with some in the Western Quarter, they dismissed his idea as an old sprite's foolishness. Despite what the others thought, Master Foote knew, beyond any shadow of a doubt, that the Green Maiden may be the only one to repel the Sorcerer Corradhu.

The Green Maiden was very concerned about Master Foote. She wasn't sure he could go on much longer. "Botsam, take Master Foote to a guest room. See that he is fed and provided a bed. Master Foote, you must rest. We will talk more in the morning. I cannot speak with you now in any event. Now, go with Botsam."

"Thank you, Mistress. I really do not feel well."

After Botsam and Master Foote left, the Green Maiden summoned another one of the guardians, Nerida.

The Green Maiden paced anxiously as she delivered her instructions. "Nerida, go at once to Clonfert House. Go to the Headmaster. Inform him that we have a messenger from the Western Quarter who seeks my help. Tell the Headmaster that the Sorcerer Corradhu is in the Western Quarter. The Headmaster has had dealings with this sorcerer before and knows the danger he presents. He has cast a powerful spell upon the spirits there making them all quite ill. Find out what the Headmaster knows about this. Ask him what he intends to do and how I might help. Impress upon him that this is urgent."

"I'm off," said Nerida as she winged her way immediately to Clonfert House.

The Green Maiden had to discover the nature of the curse. She did not think she could count on Master Foote for help. He was old, frail, sick, and she didn't want to make it worse for him. She doubted he could shed any light on the nature of the curse any way.

Once again, her thoughts turned to the Oracle of the Dar Lantern. The Green Maiden could not spare the time to go the Oracle herself. Would the Oracle come to her? The Green Maiden couldn't remember ever hearing of the Oracle setting foot outside the confines of the Cave of the Dar Lantern. If she would agree to come to the Green Maiden, then maybe the Oracle could help with the curse. Hopefully the Oracle could also advise the Green Maiden on how to proceed with Affey. There was only one way to find out.

"Spark," she called up into the branches to another one of her guardians. "Come down here. I have an errand for you."

Spark was there in a flash. "Yes, Mistress?"

"Go at once to the Cave of the Dar Lantern. Implore the Oracle to come here. Tell the Oracle I only make this request because dire circumstances keep me from coming there. Tell the Oracle it involves the Sorcerer Corradhu. She will know who he is."

"At once," Spark said as he flew off.

The Green Maiden felt the urge to rest too. She was surprised by how tired she felt. She was always able to go days without rest. Clearly, her days as the

Green Maiden were drawing to a close. She had to set aside her thoughts and feelings. There wasn't time for that now. The Sorcerer Corradhu was out to destroy the creatures of the Western Quarter. She had to figure out the nature curse. There had to be an antidote. The Green Maiden went to her library to consult the few books she had on curses. Green Maiden's didn't impose curses. They repelled them, defeated them, crushed them. The Green Maiden had never heard of a curse that was so powerful that spirits could not resist it. She had to find out if her books held the answer.

Meanwhile, Affey woke up when she heard the Green Maiden call for Spark. When Affey made her way down through the tree to where she thought the voices came from, she found it empty. Everything was still and quiet. Perhaps she was dreaming. Affey went back up into the tree to her bed. No sooner had she fallen asleep than a fierce dream came upon her. She wasn't sure where the dream took her. It was a desolate land. It was dark and moody. Queer sounds echoed. Wings fluttered desperately in the distance. Death roamed everywhere. There was a voice. A man's voice. It was icy, haunting. The dream was overcast with a foreboding atmosphere. It all seemed more real than dream. Affey woke in a sweat. Her heart was pounding. She struggled to breathe. "It's only a dream," she said to herself, over and over again, until she fell back into a dreamless sleep.

Meanwhile, the Green Maiden was in the library searching her books waiting for her messengers to return. Spark returned first.

"Good news, Mistress. The Oracle will be here mid-morning tomorrow. The Oracle wanted to spend some time in the cave consulting the Dar Lantern before coming to see you. The Oracle wanted me to assure you that, though no Oracle had even been away from the Cave of Dar Lantern, the presence of the Sorcerer Corradhu was indeed dire."

"Thank you, Spark, you may go."

"Mistress, if I may. You look worried. Is there anything I and the other guardians can do?"

"The time will soon be upon us where I will need your help. For now, rest. That is how you can help."

"Very well, Mistress. I will wait to be summoned." Spark flew back up into the branches.

The Green Maiden was anxious to hear from Nerida. Was she delayed? Had something befallen her? She was usually her quickest messenger. The

Green Maiden focused her consciousness in the direction of the Headmaster's study at Clonfert House. She was relieved to find Nerida in conference with the Headmaster, Professor O'Riley, and Michael, Kevin, and Affey's twin sister, Minda. They must be planning something. Nerida would return soon enough with the details. She must return to her books to find a remedy to the curse the Sorcerer Corradhu placed on the Western Quarter. Not one of her books was helpful.

Chapter 4
The Western Quarter the Sorcerer Corradhu's Encampment

"I Summon the Eleven Sisters of the Coven," the Sorcerer Corradhu called out to the dark, pre-dawn sky above the ritual clearing he created in the middle of his fortress in the Western Quarter. His voice carried over the treetops to reach each of the Eleven Sisters of the Coven at their various posts in the quarter. It was the hour before dawn on the fifth day. The Sorcerer Corradhu needed to perform the ritual of the curse before sunrise just as he had done every day since arriving in the Western Quarter. The curse only held if the ritual was recited each day at precisely the same time. All the Eleven Sisters of the Coven must be present. They each had a role to play. The Sorcerer Corradhu preferred the hour before dawn even though the ritual strongly suggested it be performed at midnight. He believed the pre-dawn stillness made the curse especially powerful. He was proved right when, on the morning of the second day, birds were singing. It so displeased him and so distracted him from his duties to the ritual that he struck them all down dead from their perches. Not a single bird has come again to his encampment.

One by one the Eleven Sisters of the Coven arrived back from their posts and took their places in a circle around the altar platform in the middle of the clearing. It was on this altar that the ritual for the curse played out. When he arrived in the Western Quarter, the Sorcerer Corradhu had a vision of where he would encamp. When he saw their present location, he immediately seized it from a small band of elves. He didn't harm them then. He saved that for later. He carved out this clearing in the middle the dense, pine forest. It would serve as his fortress in the Western Quarter. The Sorcerer Corradhu loved the scent of pine. It reminded him of his homeland in Sardinia, the Su Nuraxi. He cleared at large area in the center of the forest. He placed a massive granite altar on a raised platform in the clearing. It was on this altar that the ritual was performed.

Once the eleventh sister took her place in the circle, the Sorcerer Corradhu appeared in the sky above them. It was a deliberate display of his power. It was intended to remind the Eleven Sisters of the Coven that they owed all to him. The moment the first breeze announced his pending arrival, the Eleven Sisters of the Coven began to chant:

> *All hail to you*
> *Father, Corradhu.*
> *Bring us the soil*
> *From Su Nuraxi.*
> *Punish this land,*
> *Curse these spirits.*
> *Show us the way,*
> *We will follow.*
> *Punish this land,*
> *Curse these spirits.*
> *Punish this land,*
> *Curse these spirits.*

The Eleven Sisters of the Coven continued their chanting until the Sorcerer Corradhu floated down from the sky and took his place at the altar. He raised his sapphire staff ceremoniously in the air. The Eleven Sisters of the Coven stopped their chant. Torches all around the perimeter of the clearing ignited. The entire forest was cloaked in a golden light.

"My daughters, my witches, a very good morning to you all. Our destiny continues for yet another day. Praise to our ancestors at the Su Nuraxi!"

"Praise to our ancestors at the Su Nuraxi," the Eleven Sisters of the Coven responded.

The Sorcerer Corradhu was a magnificent, though malignant vision. He stood over six feet tall. He was thin and muscular. His hair, which cascaded down his back to the ground, was obsidian black. It glistened with a blue sheen that matched his sapphire staff. He was clean shaven. His eyes were just as black as his hair. His warm, bronze skin was perfect, not a single blemish. One could not tell his age. Age was beyond him. He moved with a grace that belied his terrible nature. His robe was in stark contrast to his dark visage. Unlike every previous leader of the Su Nuraxi coven who dressed entirely in black, the Sorcerer Corradhu always wore white. When he ascended to the throne as the leader of the coven, the Sorcerer Corradhu chose white as an act of defiance to the old ways. His long, white robe was made of the finest linen. It was as gossamer as swan's feathers. His waist was cinched with a belt inlaid with the finest crystals. The Sorcerer Corradhu was aware that, if the coven was to survive in the new world order of spirits and humans, a new approach was needed. It would start with their appearance. White was less threatening than the traditional black. The white would camouflage his cruel intentions.

All the witches in the coven of Su Nuraxi were required by the Sorcerer Corradhu to also dress in simple white, but with no adornments. Those in the coven who protested were banished forever. He never wore any covering on his feet, yet his bare feet were never soiled no matter where he treaded. The sound of his voice was seductive. Like cellos and violins. The Sorcerer Corradhu could not, would not, be ignored, nor would he go unnoticed. To be in his presence was to surrender to him. There was no other choice.

Before starting the ritual for the curse, he addressed the Eleven Sisters of the Coven.

"Today, our fifth day here in the Western Quarter, we must once more renew our efforts to dominate this realm. Someday soon we will subdue all the realms, spirit, and human. It is my destiny. We do not wish to annihilate the creatures who abide here. Some of you must remember this. Some of you are too eager to inflict deadly harm. We must subdue them, not kill them. They must fear us. Without them under our dominion, we cannot rule the elements here and, eventually, the elements of every realm. The curse we cast again this day shall make them a bit sicker than they were yesterday. So, it shall be every day until this realm is ours alone. They must understand that there is no antidote to this curse except my benevolence. Until their leaders surrender to me, we shall continue this curse each day. Each day it shall affect these creatures with more intensity. They will get sicker and sicker until they surrender. Do you understand?" The Sorcerer Corradhu looked each of the Eleven Sisters of the Coven in the eye. They could not resist him. Each responded the same way.

"I am yours to command, father Corradhu."

The Sorcerer Corradhu then began the ritual to extend the curse for another day.

"Is the elf ready," he asked the Eleven Sisters of the Coven.

One of them, Rosalia by name, shoved an elf toward the altar. He was a young elf. Maybe twenty years old. The elf who was used for the yesterday's ritual died during the night from the torture the Sorcerer Corradhu inflicted on him. This new elf was, like the one before him, shackled about the hands, feet, and neck. A leather mask was bound across his tiny mouth. His wings had been crudely chopped from his body leaving open wounds. He trembled with fear. Tears streaked down his cheeks. He was placed atop a small, granite block in the center of the altar. His chains were fastened to each of the small granite block's four corners. The Sorcerer Corradhu stood above him without looking at him. He was merely a sacrifice for the Sorcerer's ambition.

The Sorcerer Corradhu then called for the other sisters to bring the ritual items to the altar. One brought fresh belladonna blossoms. Four others placed a burning torch on the four corners of the massive granite altar. Another placed a toad, also in chains, on the elf's chest. The toad tried to croak an objection, but the Sorcerer Corradhu slapped it into silence. Two sisters stood beside the Sorcerer Corradhu and placed a blood red robe on his shoulders. It too was embroidered with the same crystals as his belt. Another sister held his hair back to make sure that his black mane remained outside the robe, falling beautifully to the ground. It was as if the Sorcerer Corradhu was cloaked in stars on a fiery sky. The last two sisters of the coven lit incense buckets and circled the altar with them, the fragrant smoke filling the air. The poor, chained elf struggled against his shackles to no avail.

"The moment has arrived, my sisters. I will now cast the curse for another day."

The Sorcerer Corradhu stared down menacingly at the elf. He wanted the elf's terror to overwhelm him. It did. The Eleven Sisters of the Coven began to circumambulate the altar. They kept an exact space between them, walking a slow, steady pace. They chanted quietly, "Punish this land, curse these spirits."

While the Eleven Sisters of the Coven walked round and round the altar, the Sorcerer Corradhu cast the curse.

First, he withdrew a small pouch from his crystal belt. It contained the mystical soil from the Su Nuraxi. He sprinkled it on the elf's hands and feet.

As he did, The Sorcerer Corradhu also chanted, "Punish this land, Curse this elf." Next, the Sorcerer Corradhu picked up the toad and slit its throat. He held the toad over the elf and dripped the toad's blood in three small, concentric circles on his forehead, all the while continuing the chant in unison with the Eleven Sisters of the Coven. The elf was revolted by the toad's blood. Despite having his mouth bound, he let out a cry. The Sorcerer Corradhu slapped him silent just as she had slapped the toad.

The Sorcerer Corradhu leaned over close to the elf, his lips nearly touching the elf's tiny mouth. "Utter another sound and you shall share the toad's fate." The elf's eyes widened with fright. "I do not wish to kill you, elf, but I will if necessary." The Eleven Sisters of the Coven continued their steady pace and chanting.

To reinforce his threat to the elf, the Sorcerer Corradhu raised his sapphire staff to the sky. The elf watched shaking with fear of what might happened next. The sapphire staff in the Sorcerer Corradhu's right hand began to glow. In the sky above the clearing, a lone hawk circled. The Sorcerer Corradhu reached down and took the belladonna blossoms in his left hand offering them to the sky. As he held it aloft, the hawk's wings failed. It plummeted from the sky crashing onto the elf's chest knocking the breath from them both. The elf thought the hawk was dead. The elf watched as the Sorcerer Corradhu stroked the hawk gently with the belladonna blossoms reviving it. The hawk took wing again into the sky. The elf feared he would suffer as the hawk did, only he would not be revived. The Sorcerer Corradhu leaned close to the elf once more. "That was a warning to you, elf."

The Eleven Sisters of the Coven ceased circling the altar. They stood silently facing the Sorcerer Corradhu, the altar, and the terrified elf.

The Sorcerer Corradhu began the final elements of the ritual of the curse.

"You, elf, will be the first test of our curse today. I am going to remove the binding from your mouth. Heed my warning. Do not make a sound." The Sorcerer Corradhu undid the leather binding from the elf's tiny mouth. The elf remained silent. The Sorcerer Corradhu picked up the belladonna blossoms.

"By the power of all who came before me and all who will follow, I curse this elf and all the spirits who dwell in this, the Western Quarter." As he spoke the Sorcerer Corradhu brushed the belladonna across the elf's lips, chest, hands, feet, and the three circles of toad's blood on the elf's forehead. "Let him, and every one of them, suffer from profound sickness. May their bodies be disturbed with terrible pain. May their minds be tormented with horrible images. May they suffer without pause until they surrender to me."

The Sorcerer Corradhu fixed the elf in his black gaze once more. The elf lurched against his chains. He whimpered in pain. He was desperate to fold into himself to relive the pain that descended upon him. His mind filled with the images of monsters roaming throughout the Western Quarter. They devoured every living thing in their path. The Sorcerer Corradhu released the chains from the elf's hands. The poor elf bent double clutching his stomach. The Sorcerer Corradhu released the elf's feet from their shackles. The elf drew his knees up to his chest hoping it would relieve his pain. The pain he suffered made the elf want to die.

"All of your kind will suffer as you do now. You and they will suffer endlessly until you submit to my will." The Sorcerer Corradhu seized the elf by the neck and threw him roughly to the ground knocking the breath from him once again. The elf almost passed out from the pain.

"Sister, Emelda, return this creature to his cell. Let him suffer there alone. We will bring him back tomorrow should the spirits not surrender to me and we need to perform this ritual for another day." Emelda did as she was ordered.

"Sisters, you must now scatter to your posts to watch what the spirits do today. Report to me any movement on their part to surrender. Be vigilant for any attempt to contact the other quarters for help. Now, off with you until sunset."

In his cell, which was no bigger than a bucket, the elf curled up in a corner hoping to ease his pain and subdue the awful images rushing through his mind. The wounds where his wings were severed were becoming infected. He doubted he could endure another day of this torment. If only someone would rescue him. He knew no one would or could. All his kin were suffering just as he was. Death would be better than this. Just before he drifted off to a fitful sleep, he abandoned all hope of being rescued.

The Sorcerer Corradhu returned to his private encampment deep in the pine forest. There, he sat contemplating the next steps he would take to subdue the spirits of the Western Quarter should they continue to resist him. The longer he sat in silence the greater his agitation grew. He couldn't wait for the sisters to return in the evening with their reports. He had to go see for himself how his curse was affecting the spirits of the Western Quarter. There were too many places to visit. Besides, he didn't want the Eleven Sisters of the Coven to think he didn't trust them, which he did not. He decided to visit just three villages to see how much suffering he had unleashed. He wanted to see if there was any weakening of resistance among the spirits.

First, he visited Ogrolan, a village where only sprites lived. He was pleased to see that not a single sprite was laboring in the fields. Chimneys were cold. No fires warmed the cottages. The only sounds were voices moaning in pain. He watched as one sprite attempted to take flight, but it fell hard against the ground writhing in pain. Screams were heard coming from many of the cottages he flew over. Not a single sprite child was in sight. The Sorcerer Corradhu was most pleased with what he had done.

In the village of Awearon he saw a family of knockers, a mother, father, and two children, limping toward a cave in the mountainside. The Sorcerer Corradhu noticed that other knockers were also trying to make their way to the cave, but they too struggled to walk. More than one of the knockers sat on the side of the path leading to the cave too weak to go any further. To make things worse for them, the Sorcerer Corradhu sent a cascade of boulders down the mountain to block the entrance to the cave. The knockers let out cries of pain and despair.

What pleased the Sorcerer Corradhu the most was what he watched happening in the waters of Eowiorial. The waters there were home to a tribe of kelpies. They thrashed about the lakes and ponds. They had trouble swimming. It was difficult for them to surface for a breath. They were near drowning. The Sorcerer Corradhu feared the kelpies. Being water spirits, he wondered if they would somehow be immune from his curse. Seeing them suffering as they were, proved he was wrong. No spirit was beyond his reach. *Surely*, he thought, *they would all soon surrender.*

Chapter 5
The Doon Well Major
Lisette's Encampment

Major Lisset was greeted by murmurs as she stepped onto the raised platform in the middle of the training field at the Doon Well. Her female spirit warriors had not been summoned to an assembly since the attack on Adena at Clonfert House. A general assembly was an event that usually was a prelude to battle. They wondered if they were about to engage in some new skirmish. The major had received an urgent request from the Headmaster. His messenger just departed to tell him she would honor his request.

"Sisters," Major Lisset called out as she raised her bow to silence them. Her women quieted down to hear what the Major had to say.

"I have called us all together because we have been asked for help once again by Clonfert House. It asks that we intervene in a small way in a matter that the Headmaster tells me carries the potential for grave consequences." Her troops started murmuring among themselves again.

"Sisters, please, please quiet down. I know you are itching for another adventure, but for now, I must beg you to be patient. I fear the time will soon come when your desire for a fight may soon be upon us. For now, we have been asked to undertake a small, though dangerous task. Only a few of you will be involved." The Major heard many of the women voice disappointment. None of them wished to be left out of a fight. She ignored them.

"The Headmaster of Clonfert House has asked us to undertake a rescue mission which sounds easy enough, but be warned. This will not be easy. There are serious risks involved. We have been asked to rescue a young elf who is being held captive and tortured in the Western Quarter."

The mention of an elf being tortured aroused anger in her women. They did not hold back expressing it. One of the sergeants, Kaia, the most senior of the sergeants spoke for all the women.

"What do you mean tortured? Who would do such a thing? This doesn't sound like a rescue mission. It appears to be more of a declaration of war. A war on all of us." Shouts of 'war, war' filled the air of the training field.

"Enough," Major Lisset said angrily. "War, if there is to be one, will be joined by us only after we have carefully considered all the consequences. It is what we have always done, and what we will do again this time. Is that clear?"

"It is, major," sergeant Kaia said.

A hand raised in the back of the assembly.

"Yes, private, what is it?" asked the major.

"I assume you are going to tell us more about this and not keep it to yourself or those who are to go on this mission?"

"I can only tell you what Clonfert House has told me. This is what I know. A warlock by the name of the Sorcerer Corradhu arrived recently in the Western Quarter, which you all know is in chaos since the defeat of Adena and her generals. The Headmaster believes this sorcerer is attempting to take over the Western Quarter and subdue its spirits, if not annihilate them. This sorcerer apparently placed all the spirits of the Western Quarter under a terrible curse that causes terrible, unrelenting pain and suffering. As far as the Headmaster can determine, the curse requires the daily torturing of one of the spirits from the Western Quarter. He doesn't know why or much about the curse at all. Until he knows more, he wants to at least spare the elf currently held from any further torment. Clonfert House currently lacks the resources to rescue the elf, so he has asked us to do it."

Sergeant Kaia stepped forward again and asked, "this doesn't sound that challenging. What am I missing?"

"What we are missing, first, is information about the curse. We only know the toll that it is taking on the Western Quarter. While the Headmaster knows of the Sorcerer Corradhu, he knows nothing about this curse. This sorcerer is accompanied by eleven witches known as the Eleven Sisters of the Coven. Nothing is known about them either. They all belong to the Stregheria of the Su Nuraxi in Sardinia. The extent of their power is also unknown. So much about them and the sorcerer remains a mystery, that the leaders of Clonfert House have decided not to engage the Sorcerer Corradhu just yet. They hope that by rescuing the elf there will be some interruption in the curse that will provide more intelligence. They also hope it will disrupt the Sorcerer Corradhu and the Eleven Sisters of the Coven so even more can be known about them and their power. Lastly, it is hoped that the elf can provide insight into what the Sorcerer Corradhu's intentions and plans are. That is everything I know?"

The sergeant had one more question. "You said there were serious risks with this mission. Why?"

All eyes were on Major Lisset.

"It is dangerous because I have no idea whether their powers exceed our own. If theirs do, then I fear those who undertake this mission will not return. I also fear that if this is what happens, then we will be in for a fight we may ultimately lose. The consequences of such an outcome are beyond what I, or you, should even want to consider."

"Then we must succeed," Sergeant Kaia said as she stepped back into the ranks of spirit women. The rest of the women remained silent, thinking about what the major just said.

"I need three volunteers," the major announced. All hands shot up. "Thank you, sisters, but only three may go. Sergeant Kaia, you will lead this mission. You choose who will go with you."

Sergeant Kaia stepped up onto the platform alongside Major Lisset. She asked the major privately, "are any special skills needed? Archery, sword, for example?"

"I have no idea," Major Lisset responded.

"Very well, major, I'll choose two who I believe are the most courageous and hope for the best." Sergeant Kaia looked out over the several hundred assembled warriors. As the senior sergeant, she knew every one of them. She decided on two privates.

"Private Ashira and Private Muirgen. Meet the Major and I at her tent. The rest of you increase your training effort. I think this rescue mission is only the beginning."

Major Lisset had one more thing to add to the sergeant's words. "I believe Sergeant Kaia is right. Something tells me it won't be long before we will be asked to help drive out this Sorcerer Corradhu. Train as if we fight tomorrow." The major and Sergeant Kaia adjourned to the major's tent. The rest of the women returned to their training with a new sense of purpose.

The two privates arrived quickly at the major's tent.

Sergeant Kaia spoke to them first. Major Lisset decided to let sergeant Kaia take the lead. "Private Ashira and Muirgen, if you have any reservations express them now. We cannot attempt this rescue if you have any hesitations." Each of the privates said they were fully ready. "Well, we shall depart shortly. Meet me in half an hour by the entrance to Saint Gobnait's grove." The two privates left to gather their weapons and then meet the sergeant at Saint Gobnait's grove. It was the place they always went to recite the anthems for battle.

Major Lisset interrupted the sergeant as she was about the leave. "Before you depart, sergeant, a word. I do not know what you will encounter. Here are the coordinates for the elf's location." She handed the sergeant a slip of paper. "It is a clearing in a dense wood created specifically by the Sorcerer Corradhu for the purpose of casting his curse. Somewhere on these grounds the elf is held shackled in chains in a small cage. We don't know if he is guarded or not. We don't know who may be present when you arrive. If you are outnumbered, you are to return. We cannot risk your loss."

"Don't worry, major. We will return with the elf." The sergeant left the tent. Major Lisset expected no less of a response than the sergeant gave her. Now, she had to wait.

Sergeant Kaia and the two privates made their way swiftly to the Sorcerer Corradhu's ritual clearing. They found it deserted, which gave them pause. The last thing they expected was to find an empty clearing. Why were there no lookouts or guards? Was the Sorcerer Corradhu that brazen that he would leave the elf unattended? They split up to search for the elf.

Private Muirgen found the poor elf hidden in his cage beneath the altar. She quietly lifted the cage and signaled to the elf to be quiet. She was there to rescue him. She carried the cage to the edge of the clearing. On her way, she waived to the Sergeant Kaia and Private Ashira that she had the elf. The two privates worked together silently to free him from his chains while the sergeant kept lookout. The elf was in terrible pain. His wounds were festering. Where his wings were clipped, he was developing a serious infection.

Private Muirgen used a charm to loosen the elf's shackles. Once free, Private Ashira took him into her hands and administered a tonic to ease his pain and put him to sleep. Private Muirgen re-attached the shackles to their binding rings so that it would seem as if the elf disappeared by some magic. Something she hoped the Sorcerer Corradhu would find alarming. She placed the cage back under the altar. The tour of them, the sergeant, the two privates, and the poor, wretched elf, made their way back to the Doon Well.

Despite all their efforts to relieve the elf of his pain, he succumbed to his wounds that night. Major Lisset promptly informed the Headmaster. When her troops learned of the elf's death, the major had difficulty controlling their anger. She addressed them at the elf's funeral held an hour after his passing. She decided to attend the funeral in full battle regalia.

"Sisters. The passing of this poor elf marks a turning point. We have always remained neutral in disputes between the tribes and quarters of the spirit world. But, the intrusion by this sorcerer and his witches is different. We cannot and will not sit by. I will parlay with Clonfert House since they have already decided to advance on the sorcerer and his witches. A coordinated campaign is best. For now, train with utmost intensity. I believe the fight with this sorcerer and his witches is imminent." Despite the solemnity of the elf's funeral, the women spirits let loose with a war cry.

Major Lisset's messenger arrived back from Clonfert House. "Major, the Headmaster said that he is deeply saddened by the elf's death. He sees it as an act of aggression by the Sorcerer Corradhu and the Eleven Sisters of the Coven. He asks we prepare to join them to confront and drive out these Stregerhia."

"Thank you, Tannah. Please return to your regiment. Please keep this message between us."

Major Lisset sent a messenger to the Oracle of the Dar Lantern asking for her predictions. The messenger returned with a terse response from the Oracle.

"Tell the major that she has but one day to prepare. She must join with Clonfert House. Triumph over the Sorcerer Corradhu and the Eleven Sisters of the Coven does not come easily or without costs. Lives will be lost. Tell the major I have nothing more to say."

Major Lisset was not accustomed to suffering losses. Over the centuries she had lost only a handful of women and the Oracle knew it. For the Oracle to foresee 'many losses' was deeply troubling, even though victory seemed assured. The Major decided to keep this to herself and swore the messenger to do the same. It might undermine the morale of her warriors. She did announce that she expected to move them all to Clonfert House the next day.

Chapter 6
Clonfert House, The Headmaster's Study
Minda, Michael, and Kevin Summoned

Michael, Minda, and Kevin returned to Clonfert House the Monday following the events leading to Adena's demise. Since then, the months flew by for each of them. Their integration into life as a senior student had been unremarkable, even though they were almost a decade younger than all the other students. The only obstacle they faced was some harassment from a small handful of senior students who thought these 'children' should still be back in their lower academy. Minda, more than Michael or Kevin, seemed to be the target for these older students. It was most likely due to her haughtiness, or her refusal to kowtow to them. She frequently heard them commenting on how she thought she was better than they were with her pile of books and private meetings with the Headmaster.

There was one student, in particular, Diina, a student near graduation, who took a perverse pleasure in taunting Minda. Diina was a Sammi from some remote area of Lapland, which was, to Minda's way of thinking, already remote enough. The taunting started the day Minda arrived back at Clonfert House. She would find her books misplaced. Her assignments erased from her hard drive. Minda was eventually able to identify Diina as her tormentor by Remote Viewing Diina one day while Minda was working on an assignment in the archives. Even though using her powers on a fellow student was strictly forbidden by the house rules, she broke them in this instance. Minda didn't care about the consequences.

As Minda watched, Diina entered Minda's room and rifled through her desk. Minda rushed from the library back to her room. This would be the last time Diina would harass her. Minda stood outside her door quietly waiting for Diina to open it. As soon as Diina opened the door Minda punched her hard in the stomach. Diina dropped to the floor. Minda sat on top of her, pinning her down.

"You enter my room or mess with my stuff again and I'll do more than punch you." Minda grabbed Diina by the hair and dragged her halfway down the hallway where she let go of her. Diina didn't get up. "Do not underestimate me, Diina." Minda turned her back on Diina, walked back into her room, and slammed the door. She hadn't seen Diina since. The others who taunted her kept their distance. Diina must have not reported Minda because nothing was ever said about it.

Today, as Minda walked to her class in Sacred Geometry, she was intercepted by Gianni Giannotti. She had only seen him once in the months since her return to Clonfert House.

Gianni stood in the hallway blocking her path, hands on his hips, his trademark lavender scarf draped around his neck.

"Miss Minda, how delightful to see you here as one of us." Gianni spread his arms to embrace her. Minda was having none of that this time. She was his peer now and not some junior student. He dropped his arms and put on a sad face. "Come now, Minda. We are old friends."

"Old friends or not, Giaaaaaaanni." Minda stretched out the syllables of his name, "I am no longer a junior student here. You will show me some respect." She stepped toward him. He backed up a little.

"Urumph! So much for friendship." Gianni took one, tentative step toward Minda. Her eyes dared him to come closer.

"Very well, Miss Minnnnnnda." It was Gianni's turn to elongate her name. "The Headmaster and Professor O'Riley want to see you immediately. Your companions, Michael and Kevin are also on their way there." Gianni didn't wait for Minda to respond. He tossed one end of his lavender scarf over his left shoulder and sauntered off in a huff. He mumbled something under his breath, but Minda couldn't make out his words. She watched him with a smirk on her face. It didn't matter what he was mumbling, she had put him in his place.

Minda made her way to the corridor that led to the Headmaster's study. Michael and Kevin were waiting outside the Headmaster's door. When they saw her, they ran to meet her. They hadn't seen much of each other since returning. Professor O'Riley demanded most of Michael's time in the library. Kevin was training with Professors Mbaye and Smiley which left him little time to socialize with Michael or Minda. Minda was assigned a smattering of classes, mostly math and physics related. In addition, the Headmaster required her presence in his private study every afternoon for lessons in the history of Clonfert House, the Sacred Fairy Scrolls, and other topics Michael and Kevin were not privy to.

Kevin whispered, "What have we done? Are we in trouble?" He always defaulted to thinking they were summoned for some infraction of the rules.

"Nice to see you too, Kevin," Minda said sarcastically.

"How have you been," Michael asked her as they walked back toward the Headmaster's study.

"Busy. You," she asked them both.

"Busy," Michael said.

"Busy," Kevin echoed.

"I wonder what this is all about," Minda asked.

"You are about to find out," Professor O'Riley said as he opened the door to the Headmaster's study. The three of them had forgotten how uncanny it was that the professor always knew they were just outside the door.

Given the arrival of the Sorcerer Corradhu in the Western Quarter and given the strength of the curse he unleashed on the spirits in that realm, the Headmaster wasted no time in idle chit-chat. He got right to the point of their being summoned.

"We have a serious development in the. Western Quarter."

Minda was about to interrupt him with a question.

"Minda," Professor O'Riley cut her off sharply.

"Sorry, sir, old habits."

The Headmaster continued. "Since Adena's defeat, the Western Quarter is in complete disarray. The tribes are scattered. There is no leadership. They have not suffered from an evil influence, at least until several days ago. The Sorcerer Corradhu and his Eleven Sisters of the Coven arrived from the Su Nuraxi, their home nuraghe in Sardinia. We don't have time to explain about the Su Nuraxi right now because he has placed an awful curse over the entire Wester Quarter. Every spirit in that realm is suffering terribly under the curse. They suffer intolerable physical pain together with terrible visions. We have learned that he must implement the curse each day or it loses its effect. We believe this is a weakness we can take advantage of, though we don't know how just yet. Each casting of the curse increases the spirits' torment. We fear that if we don't put a stop to the Sorcerer Corradhu soon, the tribes of the

Western Quarter will be annihilated. We learned of this just this morning. A messenger from the Green Maiden brought this news. Let me introduce you to her. Nerida, these are the enchanters I told you about."

Nerida stepped out from behind the Headmaster's chair. "I am pleased to meet you. I have told the Headmaster everything we know so far. It is bad. The Western Quarter needs your help. I will stay until I know what your plans are and then I will return to my mistress. She stands ready to assist in every way possible."

"How is my sister," Minda asked.

"Very well, Minda," Nerida said.

The Headmaster cut off any further discussion of Affey. It would distract from the urgency of dealing with the Sorcerer Corradhu.

"Unfortunately," he said, "part of the ritual for the curse requires a spirit, in this case an elf, to be subjected to the pain of the curse on the Sorcerer Corradhu's altar. This sacrificial elf is the first to suffer from the curse. With the help of Major Lisset, we have already rescued this elf while the Sorcerer Corradhu was away from his encampment roaming the Western Quarter. He will return to his encampment very soon. We don't know how he will react, but we expect the worse."

Minda interrupted the Headmaster. "If I may, Headmaster. Why is this our responsibility? Shouldn't the spirits take care of this sorcerer and his witches?"

The Headmaster had to contain his displeasure with Minda's question. He stared at her sharply. "After all I have taught you, this is what you are thinking? You know our responsibility to the spirits. Shame on you for that question."

"I am very sorry, Headmaster. I don't know why I thought that. It was impertinent of me." Minda was truly sorry.

"Lesson learned," the Headmaster said.

"What do you want from us," Minda asked sheepishly.

"We will get to that in a minute," Professor O'Riley said.

Kevin's leg started shaking as it always did when he was anxious. Michael didn't react at all, but he didn't like the fact that, once again, they were being called upon to face off with a challenge. Why was it that only they could overcome this threat even though they were young, inexperienced enchanters? Having seen the Headmaster's reaction to Minda's question, Michael held his tongue.

"We have a task for each of you. They are part of our plan to eventually confront the Sorcerer Corradhu. You are exempted from your classes for the time being. You must keep what you are told and what you are doing secret. I don't have to remind you of the necessity." The Headmaster looked to Minda knowing that she would have a question. "Go ahead, Minda, ask."

"What about the other students? We are not isolated like we were before. They will know our routines are different. They will be suspicious."

"We don't have time to worry about that. Just ignore them. And, Minda, don't punch anyone," the Headmaster said with a grin.

Michael and Kevin looked at Minda. What had she done now?

The Headmaster assigned Kevin his task first. "Kevin, I want you to go into the woods adjacent to the eastern turret. Make sure you go far enough away so that you cannot be seen. Once there, I want you use your Transcendental Movement skills to practice weaving the trees, bushes, and other vegetation there into an inescapable dome surrounded by an impenetrable wall that will confine anything caught in it. This should be easier than transporting the river water into the basement of Saint Brendan's Cathedral as you did before."

Whenever Kevin was asked to deploy one of his powers, it erased all doubt in himself. His powers were the one confident thing about him. His leg stopped shaking.

"Yes, Headmaster. Shall I go now," Kevin asked.

"Wait until I'm finished with the three of you. All of you need to know what the other are being asked to do." The Headmaster then explained to Minda what was expected of her.

"Minda, I need you to Consciousness Mirror the Sorcerer Corradhu if you can. I suspect it might be difficult, if not impossible. I encountered him myself long ago. He is a mighty opponent. If you cannot, then try Remote Viewing. I don't think that will be too hard for you. He is most likely distracted with the impact of his curse to detect you. Either way, I need you to monitor him in any way that you can. You will do it from here, in my study. I need to know everything as it unfolds."

Minda sat waiting for the Headmaster to direct her to begin. She thought of her sister, Affey. Would Affey play a role in all of this? How was her sister? They had not said a word to each other since Affey left to join the Green

Maiden all those months ago. Minda really wanted to corner Nerida and ask her about Affey. That was not going happen.

Professor O'Riley then spoke to Michael.

"Michael, you, and I are going to the secret library. We have to find any references to this curse that the Sorcerer Corradhu placed on the Western Quarter."

Michael had not anticipated anything like this. He was strictly forbidden to enter the secret library even though he was tapped to be Professor O'Riley's successor as the librarian of Clonfert House. Professor O'Riley repeatedly reminded Michael that it would be several years before he would have any access to the secret library. Michael was so taken aback by this they he had nothing to say to the professor. Professor O'Riley and Michael left for the secret library. The Headmaster sent Kevin off to the woods to practice. Minda and the Headmaster were alone.

"I have one more question before I start, Headmaster," Minda said.

"Yes, Minda."

"Is my sister, Affey, involved in all of this? Is she okay? When will I see her?"

"That's three questions, Affey." The Headmaster pointed out.

"Yes, your sister is involved as we all will be. She is doing very well. I'm afraid it will be some time before you and your sister can visit. Now, please begin. It is most important that I know what you are capable of with the Sorcerer Corradhu." Nerida interrupted.

"Headmaster, I must return now to the Green Maiden. I will inform her of what you are planning. I am sure that she will contact you soon to find out what further plans you have and how she can help." Nerida vanished through the Headmaster's window.

The Headmaster sat at his desk reading an oversized, leather bound volume about curses waiting for Minda to report the success of her efforts to either Consciousness Mirror or Remote View the Sorcerer Corradhu.

Minda tried mirroring the Sorcerer Corradhu's consciousness, but she failed. She finally was able to Remote View him, but what she saw faded in and out of view. Even when she was able to see, the view was hazy, at best. What she was able to see was that the Sorcerer Corradhu was making his way back to his encampment.

"He's heading back," she announced to the Headmaster.

"Keep your eyes on him, Minda," the Headmaster ordered. "I am going to the forest to check on Kevin. If you need me for anything let me know. I won't be long."

Chapter 7
The Eo Mugna Tree
Affey's Transformation Begins The Oracle
of the Dar Lantern Visits

The sun broke warm and bright the next morning. The Oracle of the Dar Lantern was visiting today. The seven guardians of the Eo Mugna Tree were already awake with excitement for the Oracle's visit. No one of the Oracle's importance or stature had ever come to the Eo Mugna Tree before. They sensed her arrival before the Green Maiden did. As they scurried down from their perches high up in the tree to greet her, they made quite a racket. They pushed and shoved each other trying to be the first to greet the Oracle. They made such a racket that Affey awoke from a deep sleep. As she wiped the sleep from her eyes, she noticed something quite peculiar.

She first noticed it on her fingers. Affey, a descendent of African Enchanters, had what she liked to describe as 'chocolate skin'. What she saw this morning was a green shadow just below the surface of her 'chocolate skin'. It was barely visible. She stroked each of her fingers to see if the green would disappear at her touch. If anything, her touch made the green brighter. The pale, emerald green was spreading everywhere under her brown skin. She turned her hand over to look at her palms. They were no longer cream colored. They had turned a very pale shade of green. She watched amazed as her arms turned the same shade of pale, emerald green. She lifted her night shirt and watched as the green slowly spread down her legs. She curled her toes as the green reached them. It tickled a little. She covered her legs back up with her night shirt and closed her eyes. *Maybe,* she thought, *I'm still sleeping and this is a dream.* After several minutes she opened her eyes again. This was no dream. Her fingers were still tinted emerald green. Her arms legs were the same. She jumped out of bed and ran to the mirror. Sure enough, her face was changing color too. She slowly ran the tips of her fingers over her face. She giggled at the green on her cheeks. There were a few, barely visible, strands of gold in the curls of her dreadlocks. Her eyes too were different, though she couldn't tell what color they were becoming. She thought to herself, *and, so it begins.* Affey was so anxious to show the Green Maiden what was happening, that she forgot all about the ruckus the seven guardians caused. She dressed quickly. Something was different here too. Her dress was too long. Yesterday it fit her perfectly. Was she getting smaller? She had to show the Green Maiden.

"Mistress, mistress," Affey called out excitedly as she sprang from her bedroom to rush through the branches toward the Green Maiden's living room. She burst in, then stopped abruptly. Her mouth hung open. Her eyes widened. The Oracle of the Dar Lantern was sitting with the Green Maiden by the hearth. She heard about the Oracle at Saint Brendan's Academy. Affey had seen pictures of the Oracle, but never met anyone who had actually seen the Oracle. The Oracle was treated as a mystery never to be solved. Yet, there was The Oracle of the Dar Lantern sitting in the Green Maiden's living room.

The Oracle immediately noticed the green of Affey's complexion. "Hello, Affey." The Oracle said. "My, oh my, you have changed," She was pleased to see that Affey's transformation had begun. The Green Maiden did not see it at first. She was too preoccupied with the Oracle's presence.

"Affey, this is the Oracle of…" the Green Maiden started to say.

"I know who this is," Affey interrupted as she walked confidently toward the Oracle offering her right hand for a shake.

"As I was about to say, Affey, this is the Oracle of the Dar Lantern. She is here to help me, to help us."

The Oracle shook Affey's hand. Affey didn't want to let go. The Oracle's hand was warm and strong. Then, the Green Maiden saw what was happening to Affey.

"Oh! Affey dear! It seems it has begun." The Green Maiden motioned Affey to come close to her. She examined Affey in much the same way that Affey had examined herself. The Green Maiden touched Affey's cheek. She held out Affey's arms to see the full effect of the green on Affey's skin. She softly stroked the first, few strands of gold in Affey's hair.

"Affey, this is just the beginning. I'm sorry I didn't tell you about this. I assumed it would be sometime yet before this would begin. I thought I had more time to prepare you. I just have to accept that you are transforming much quicker than I expected." The Green Maiden's voice was anxious, but neither the Oracle not Affey said anything about it.

The Oracle of the Dar Lantern said to the Green Maiden and Affey, "you both must accept that this transition of Green Maidens. You, Affey becoming the eighth Green Maiden. You, Green Maiden, leaving us. Both are quickening." The Oracle said to the Green Maiden, "you must not delay her training. Do you understand?"

"I do," said the Green Maiden. She was once again faced with the fact that her time as Green Maiden was drawing to a close. More importantly, the Oracle just told the Green Maiden that she had very little time to bring Affey into her full Green Maidenhood. She harbored serious doubts about her ability to finish Affey's transformation.

The Oracle then spoke to Affey. "Affey, your transformation as the eighth Green Maiden comes at a difficult time. We will expect more of you than is probably fair, but, then again, when more was expected of you before you rose to the occasion. I have no doubt you will once again."

"I know, Oracle. It seems it is my destiny to be called upon earlier than I should. I am thankful I have the two of you to guide me."

"Not me," the Oracle corrected Affey. "I am here to advise the Green Maiden. You are joined to her, not me."

The Green Maiden saw that Affey was disappointed. "Affey, the Oracle only means there are responsibilities at the Cave of the Dar Lantern that cannot be ignored. The Oracle will help us when we need it." Affey seemed relieved. "Now, the Oracle and I need some private time. I have asked the guardians to demonstrate some of their skills to you. I want you to become acquainted with how they guard the Eo Mugna Tree. I also want them to show you some of the more hidden parts of our forest. Botsam!" she called out.

"Yes, mistress," Botsam said from the entry way to the living room. He had been waiting to be called.

"Please show Affey what we discussed. Bring her back in an hour. Affey, go with Botsam. I think you will have some fun."

As soon as Affey and Botsam departed, the Green Maiden and the Oracle turned to the subject of Affey's transformation. The Oracle spoke first.

"Affey is a remarkable girl. You worry about her needlessly."

"Oracle, she is a mortal. I am fay. I am not sure I know enough about humans to know where to start. I read through the Annals of the Sisterhood, but there was nothing there to help. She doesn't know anything about being fay. I just don't see how I can make this happen." The Green Maiden was near tears.

The Oracle leaned over taking the Green Maiden's hands in hers. "You must trust yourself. Do you hear me?" The Oracle needed to snap the Green Maiden out of her mood.

"I suppose." Doubt was overtaking the Green Maiden. She was growing tired.

"Stop! Enough of this doubt."

The Oracle had something to tell the Green Maiden that might help. The Oracle had not planned on sharing it during this visit. The Oracle thought it would be better to wait to tell her later, but seeing the Green Maiden's distress, the Oracle decided now was as good a time as any.

"I learned something during my contemplation in the Cave of the Dar Lantern before coming here that will give you hope."

"What might that be," the Green Maiden asked.

"Affey is the rarest of creatures. Yes, she is mortal, but she is one of one of the rare ones, an enchanter. This sets her apart from the rest of her kind. You must keep that in mind. Many years ago, during one of my daily consultations with the Dar Lantern, I foresaw Affey as the eighth Green Maiden. Perhaps not Affey in particular, but my vision foretold of her arrival. No date or time was given. Since we both know your time to depart is coming, it comes as no surprise to me that Affey is the one I saw in my visions. So, when you called for me, I knew what I would find when I came. There is also a prophecy about her. As you just witnessed, she has already started her transformation. Here is the part of my vision that should give you comfort. You, my dear friend, will succeed in transforming her."

"Why this girl? Why now?" asked the Green Maiden. The Green Maiden was so anxious and didn't hear the Oracle's comment about the prophecy. The Oracle didn't say anything more about it.

The Oracle paused and looked away in thought. When the Oracle turned back to the Green Maiden the Oracle said, "it is time for humans to take more responsibility. The fay must step back for a while. Yes, you and your kind must remain present and vigilant in the world, but if the world is to thrive, the mortals must assume some of the responsibility. It will take Affey, part human, part fay, to lead them."

"How can you say that?" The Green Maiden feared what such a development would mean for the earth. Was this to be the end of the fay? Was Affey the final Green Maiden? What would become of the wind and the woods?

"I know what you're thinking, Green Maiden. Don't forget I can see all. No, this is not the end of anything. It just a beginning. It all begins with you and Affey. The Dar Lantern reveals that she will oversee the shift of the care of the earth from fay to human. It is why she was chosen. She is the bridge to the future. It will not be easy for her. There may be resistance from both realms. How much, if any, remains to be seen. She will succeed, but It will take most her five hundred years as Green Maiden for it to be completed."

"Are you sure about all of this," the Green Maiden asked.

"The Dar Lantern is never wrong," replied the Oracle.

"Then what do I do? The stakes are too high for me to fail." The Green Maiden got up from her chair and walked over to a window that overlooked the forest. The Oracle followed her. They stood together looking out over the world they both loved. A soft breeze came through the window.

"Do not be afraid, Green Maiden. The Dar Lantern also showed me just how well you will do in transforming her. It revealed to me that Affey would be revered over future generations by fay and human alike. You and she will be memorialized as the ones who preserved and protected the world as it truly is." The Green Maiden rested her head on the Oracle's shoulder. The Oracle waited. The Green Maiden gathered herself.

"Thank you, Oracle. I will just have to trust my instincts, trust Affey's instincts. We will get through this together."

"Yes, you will. Now. We should talk about the Sorcerer Corradhu."

Chapter 8

The Western Quarter The Sorcerer Corradhu's Discovery

The Sorcerer Corradhu was in no hurry to return to his encampment. He was taking time to relish the havoc his curse unleashed on the spirits of the Western Quarter. Their unending torment would soon lead to their surrender. Of this, he was certain. Before he went to his private encampment, he stopped at the ritual clearing ground. He enjoyed a post-curse visit to relish in his power. He also wanted to check on the elf to make sure he was still alive. He didn't want to have procure a new spirit for tomorrow's ritual.

The elf's small cell was still locked tight, but the elf was gone.

"What magic is this," he said aloud angrily. He looked around to see if any creature was lurking nearby. The clearing was empty. There was not a sound to be heard other than the wind through the pines. He reached into his belt and pulled out his key to the small cell. Before he unlocked it, he examined the lock for any signs that it had been compromised. He could not find any scratches or marks suggesting that it had been tampered with. Everything seemed to be in order as far as the security of the cage was concerned. Even inside the cage, things were as they should be, except the elf had vanished. The elf's chains were still locked in place as if they bound a ghost. They were still attached to the rings on the floor. Somehow, someone, entered the cell and released the elf without unlocking his shackles. Or, through some other mischief, the elf escaped on his own. The Sorcerer Corradhu closed the cell door, locked it, and went back to the altar where he stood going back over all the elements he performed during the morning's ritual of the curse.

"Did I miss some element of the ritual? Was I not sincere enough in speaking the required words? No," he assured himself, "I performed the ritual perfectly as I always do." The Sorcerer Corradhu always blamed someone else for anything that failed. Yet, he was quick to take credit for any success even if he had nothing do with it. "It must be one of the Eleven Sisters of the Coven. One of them must have had pity on the elf. She betrayed me. I will find out which one of them it is." He spoke loudly so that any creature or sister who might be listening would hear his threat. He proclaimed even louder.

"I, the Sorcerer Corradhu, will severely punish the sister who did this. I will make her an example to the others. She will be publicly tortured, then sent back to the Su Nuraxi for perpetual imprisonment." He listened for any sound from the forest. Silence. It seemed no creatures were nearby. It angered him even more.

He was deeply troubled by the elf's escape for another reason. If the spirits of the Western Quarter did not surrender to him today, which appeared unlikely with each passing hour, then he would need a new spirit for tomorrow's ritual. "Not a problem," he assured himself, "there are more than enough sprites, elves, and their kind for sacrificing." He had an idea of how to secure a new spirit and ferret out the sister responsible for the elf's escape. Rather than wait for the Eleven Sisters of the Coven to return in the evening, he summoned them back immediately. In his haste to blame one of the witch sisters, he refused to consider any other explanation.

The Sorcerer Corradhu raised his sapphire staff and called out into the sky above, "Sisters of the Coven. Return at once. I have need of your presence." He waited angrily at the altar for them to return. His rage was growing.

Three sisters located near each other at their assigned posts heard his call. They decided to return together. Along the way, they tried to guess as to why he was summoning them back now before it was time to return.

"Something must have happened," Assunta said.

"I didn't notice anything happening with the spirits did you," Livia asked the other sisters.

"I didn't notice anything either. They were in more pain than yesterday as expected. There were no signs of a movement to surrender," replied Leonora.

"There must have been some communication from the spirits. Why else would we be called back? This is a good sign," Livia suggested.

Assunta had reservations. "I'm not so sure about that. If there were envoys sent to the Sorcerer about surrendering, then he would have entertained them by himself. No matter what the spirits offered, he would demand more. The spirits would be detained while he waited for our evening reports to see if there were other signs of submission. I have this feeling that we are being called back because something bad has happened."

"We won't have to wait long to find out. We're back," said Leonora.

The three sisters were the last to arrive. Like the others who arrived before them, each paid their respects to the Sorcerer Corradhu by taking a knee before him then kissing him on both cheeks. None of the Eleven Sisters of the Coven saw anything in the Sorcerer Corradhu's appearance that spelled trouble. He had his anger under control, if only briefly. Once the Eleven Sisters of the Coven settled around the altar the Sorcerer Corradhu spoke.

"You are probably surprised that I have brought you back so soon from your posts." Nothing in his voice suggested that the Eleven Sisters of the Coven should be worried.

"Yes, father, we are," they all responded.

Assunta, the eldest of the sisters, asked him, "has something happened? Have the spirits said they will submit to you?"

The Sorcerer Corradhu looked at Assunta with eyes darker than usual. Assunta wondered, *why is he looking at me with such intensity?* Something was wrong. She knew it in her bones.

"No, Assunta, they have not." His voice carried a threat.

The Eleven Sisters of the Coven were scared. They had seen the Sorcerer Corradhu when he was angry. When he was, one of them would have to pay the price.

The Sorcerer Corradhu then placed the elf's small, empty bucket-like cage on the altar. When he did, the Eleven Sisters of the Coven gasped. They could see that the elf's chains were intact and still attached to the rings on the floor of the cage, but the elf was gone. From the way the sorcerer was acting, it was obvious that he was not the reason the elf was gone from his cage. The Sorcerer Corradhu let the implications of the elf's escape sink in. The Eleven Sisters of the Coven did not know what they should do. The Sorcerer Corradhu wasted no time in telling them.

"One of you is responsible for this," the Sorcerer Corradhu said holding the cage aloft. The menace in his voice pierced each one of the witch sisters. They immediately professed their innocence.

"It is not me," some of them yelled.

"None of us would do such a thing," others said.

"It must be the spirits," still others shouted.

"Could it be those mortals from Clonfert House," one of them shouted.

The Sorcerer Corradhu raised his left hand to silence them.

"No spirit would dare to set foot inside this clearing. The humans are all cowards. They would not dare to confront me. No, sisters, it is one of you. I will find out who it is." He looked over the eleven witches who surrounded him. Not a single sister had ever disobeyed him. None had ever betrayed him. This time one of them had. He refused to entertain any another reason for the elf's disappearance.

"Either the one responsible comes forward now, or I will take measures to find out who you are." He waited for one of them to step forward. None of them did. He changed his tone. He would ferret out the traitor another way.

"Very well, then, I have an immediate assignment for each of you. We will deal with the matter of the traitor among you later."

The Eleven Sisters of the Coven felt they were given a momentary reprieve. Not one of them believed that there was a traitor among them. They didn't see that the Sorcerer Corradhu's plan was a trap.

"Each of you is to scour your respective areas of the Western Quarter for a new sacrificial spirit. You must choose very, very carefully. You must bring me back one that you guarantee cannot escape. When you have all returned, each of you will present your sacrificial spirit to me You will explain to me why it is not capable of escaping. I will choose one of them for the ritual of the curse. Once chosen, the sister who brought me the spirit will swear, on penalty of her own life, that her spirit will not escape." The Eleven Sisters of the Coven were never threatened with their lives by anyone in the coven, sorcerer or not. Wanting to instill even more fear in them he said, "Only this time, the sacrifice will be a final one for the spirit. It will not to live for a second day. It will be killed."

This was more terrifying than anything the Sorcerer Corradhu had ever said. He told them just that morning that killing a spirit was forbidden. Why had he changed his mind? What danger was ahead for the witches themselves? He wouldn't harm them as long as the elf's disappearance could be explained. The Sorcerer Corradhu would take care of them as he always had. It was his sacred duty. They only had to find a way to convince him that none of them betrayed him. Assunta was the only one who suspected just how serious the Sorcerer Corradhu was. She alone knew that one of them, guilt or not, would be sacrificed along with the elf.

Assunta was the oldest and most experienced of the Eleven Sisters of the Coven. She had been a sister under two of the previous sorcerers. Her mother and grandmother had also been sisters of the coven. If Assunta's memory served her correctly, never had a sister betrayed a sorcerer. For a sorcerer to even suggest betrayal by a witch sister was too much for her. What flaw in him did such a thing point to? What should she do? She could return immediately to the Su Nuraxi and inform the secretariat of what was happening here. However, if she was wrong, she would be banished from the coven forever. On the other hand, if the secretariat believed her, then there would be a confrontation between them and the Sorcerer Corradhu which could be catastrophic for all. She then thought of a way to save her sisters, even if it meant her having to flee the coven.

If the Sorcerer Corradhu needed someone to blame, then let it be me, Assunta decided. If she didn't return with a sacrificial spirit as he ordered, then it would be all the proof he would need to place the blame on her. It would save the other witch sisters. Of course, it would mean the end of her own sisterhood. Her name and the names of her ancestors would be struck from the history of the coven. If the Sorcerer Corradhu was on a dangerous path, perhaps it would be better to sacrifice herself for the good of all. Could she find a way to stop him? There was no time to consider all her options. She had to act now. She knew what she had to do and where she had to go.

Assunta waited until five of the sisters departed before she left. She didn't want to draw any attention to herself by leaving first, or last. Once away from the Sorcerer Corradhu, she flew to the only place she could go.

Back in the Headmaster's study at Clonfert House, Minda continued Remote Viewing the Sorcerer Corradhu. She took detailed notes of everything she witnessed. She wanted to make sure the Headmaster was fully informed. As she watched and took notes, her attention was briefly drawn to one of the witches. While all the other witches flew off to the west, this witch took off due north. Since the Sorcerer Corradhu had ordered them to find a sacrificial spirit in the Western Quarter, the witch heading north seemed to be defying the order. Why north? Minda also noticed that this witch took off much faster than any of the others. It was as if this witch was running away. Was she? Was this witch running away to the north? If she was, then there is only one place she could go to be safe. Minda had to inform the Headmaster about this as soon as he returned.

Chapter 9
The Eo Mugna Tree
The Oracle's Predictions

Once Affey and Botsam departed to meet the other guardians for their little adventure, the Oracle of the Dar Lantern led the Green Maiden to a spot a short distance from the Ego Mugna Tree. The Oracle didn't want the energy of the tree to interfere with what she had to share with the Green Maiden.

"Dear friend, let us sit down here." The Green Maiden sat on the ground. The Oracle sat with her back up against the trunk of a tree, facing the Green Maiden. The Oracle wished that what the Dar Lantern revealed was all happy news. Judging from the Oracle's countenance, the Green Maiden feared that what she was about to learn was going to be difficult to hear.

The Oracle said, "let me first try to put you at ease for I see you are anticipating bad news."

"I am Oracle, I am," said the Green Maiden.

"Not everything I have to tell you is bad, but some of it is going to be hard to hear, such is the nature of what is ahead. No matter what trials and difficulties lay ahead, when the current events have completely unfolded, Affey will step into your shoes successfully. Never forget that. There will be times when you will have your doubts. Rest assured that she will succeed. The truth is, there is much that will happen to test her and test you. You know, Green Maiden, your time here is almost over, don't you?"

"I do," the Green Maiden said sadly. "It is the way of the life of a Green Maiden. I only wish there would be enough time to prepare Affey."

"There is more than enough time for Affey. However, the arrival of the Sorcerer Corradhu and his coven requires Affey to transform without any further delay. You have no choice in this regard. She must transition now. My visions from the Dar Lantern made this very clear."

The Green Maiden had plenty of doubt, particularly about her ability to transform Affey into the eighth Green Maiden. She also had far too many questions and far too many reservations about how to accomplish this in what was now a very short time.

"Oracle, my own transition took years. It was almost a century before I felt adequate as a Green Maiden. What you're telling me is that Affey has only days for her transition. That is simply beyond my capability."

The Green Maiden had never questioned her abilities before. Her own transition flowed slowly, naturally over many years. Over the course of those years, she had time to practice her skills. Her predecessor, the sixth Green Maiden, enjoyed the luxury of time to adequately prepare her. Now, if the Oracle's predictions were true, which they always were, then there was no time for practice or patience. Affey must transform now, this very day. The transformation had already begun on its own, as it always has. Without warning, the new Green Maiden's skin starts turning green. A few, golden strands of hair appear. It just starts unannounced. It is what happened to the Green Maiden herself. One day she woke up and there it was. A green tint spreading over her body. The Green Maiden wondered, since Affey is human and not fay, maybe her transformation will unfold differently. Regardless, the Green Maiden did not feel prepared. There was the final ritual that had to be performed by all the former Green Maidens and Spirit Sisters. How on earth could the Green Maiden send word for them to assemble now?

"Oracle, can you help me? Can you guide me? This terrifies me since the whole of the Western Realm is in peril. I fear that I, Affey, or perhaps both of us, may be their only hope."

"In a sense you and Affey are their hope, but not their only hope," the Oracle of the Dar Lantern said. "You have allies at Clonfert House. There are also other spirit allies who will come to your assistance when needed." The Oracle then steered the conversation away from Affey for the time being to return to the Sorcerer Corradhu. His curse and Affey's transformation were intertwined. The Oracle had to tread carefully with the Green Maiden so that she would not become more unsure of herself than she already was.

"Let's turn our attention to the Sorcerer Corradhu, Green Maiden. He is the pivot around which all events will turn. There are things you should know about him. These are things you must share with Clonfert House if time and opportunity allow, which they may not."

"I know quite a bit about him already," the Green Maiden Said. "You make it sound as if he has some things that are hidden."

"They are not hidden. He is not like most sorcerers who rely on magic and tricks. What makes the Sorcerer Corradhu dangerous is that he doesn't follow the rules. He has no respect for traditions. When it comes to the ethics of the world of sorcery and witchcraft, he sincerely believes they do not apply to him. The Sorcerer Corradhu sees himself as transcending all rules. He is convinced that power was given to him so that he could hold dominion over all worlds. He has no scruples when it comes to achieving his goals. There is no spirit, thing, creature, or mortal he will not destroy to win. He will even go so far as to sacrifice his own coven for his personal gain. A sorcerer like Corradhu is most dangerous because of this. There are no checks on the exercise of his powers. He knows that the secretariat at the Su Nuraxi will not challenge him. They fear him the most. He would destroy them, as well, if needed. Can you see how this attitude of his is, in and of itself, dangerous?"

"Oracle, I do. I can also see where what you have described is a sorcerer with weaknesses. We can and will exploit them," the Green Maiden said too confidently.

"Don't be so sure, Green Maiden." The Oracle had to convince the Green Maiden that the Sorcerer Corradhu was no ordinary sorcerer. "A creature without a moral compass is as dangerous as one with unlimited powers. In the Sorcerer Corradhu's case, he is possessed of both. Let me tell you about the curse he is casting over the Western Quarter." The Oracle wasn't sure if the Green Maiden would believe what she had to say about the curse or not.

"The curse the Sorcerer Corradhu is casting daily has not been used for well over a thousand years. The last time it was employed, by a witch named Giuseppina. She used it to crush a tribe of gnomes. She did it for the sheer pleasure of seeing if the curse would work. Within a week's time, not only was every gnome in the area dead but so was every other creature in that place. Her curse turned a once verdant valley into a wasteland. When the secretariat at Su Nuraxi discovered what she had done, they burned her at a stake in the center of their nuraghe. All manuscripts, except the one that contained the words and ritual actions for the curse, were also burned. The lone copy of the method for casting the curse was entrusted to a sorcerer whose name and life are lost to the fog of history. No one knows what happened to him or the manuscript. It has always been assumed it was forever lost. Somehow, the Sorcerer Corradhu found it. We do know this much about the curse. The real power of the curse lies in five ritual elements without which the curse fails. The first is the use of sacred soil from the Su Nuraxi. The second one is the use of a toad's blood. The third is the Sorcerer Corradhu's sapphire staff. The fourth is a sacrificial spirit. The final element is the required presence of at least three of the witches from the Eleven Sisters of the Coven All must be present to cast the curse. What we don't know is the specific words to be said, or the actions to be employed."

The Green Maiden interrupted the Oracle. "If just one of these elements needs to be eliminated, then why haven't the spirits in the Western Quarter stopped him?"

"They don't know about this. I only learned of it myself last night during my contemplations with the Dar Lantern."

"I can dispatch Botsam and the other guardians to steal one of the items and we can finish with the Sorcerer Corradhu today," the Green Maiden said.

The Green Maiden still didn't quite understand what the Oracle was telling her. It was frustrating for the Oracle. The Oracle decided to change her approach with the Green Maiden. The Oracle became very serious and formal.

"Green Maiden, approaching the fortress of the Sorcerer Corradhu is nearly impossible. His companions and protectors, the Eleven Sisters of the Coven, have a perimeter around his fortress. They see and know all. They are powerful witches. Your guardians would suffer great losses in a confrontation with them. Even if they got past the witches, your guardians would have to face the Sorcerer Corradhu himself. They would need to capture or kill him. Quite frankly, they cannot. They will all perish."

"Then what do we do?" asked the Green Maiden.

"Because I was in a hurry to get here," the Oracle explained, "the final visions I received from the Dar lantern were murky. What I could make out in the visions was this. It will take an alliance of spirits and humans to subdue him. The curse may yet ravage more of the Western Quarter before he and his coven are driven out. Clonfert House will be at your side. I could not see more about them. Another spirit, a female who is strong, militaristic, and has her own army, will also be of help. This is probably Major Lisset, though I am not certain that it refers to her. I also saw the possibility of a defector from Corradhu's camp, but this was the murkiest of all of the visions."

"What of Affey?" asked the Green Maiden.

"Once again, the visions were not clear. Somehow, she wields great power in these events. My visions with the Dar Lantern regarding Affey were not specific. I did envision that there will be at least one loss that she will have to endure."

The Green Maiden pleaded with the Oracle, "please tell me it is not her twin sister, Minda."

"I cannot say for sure, Green Maiden. All I saw was more than one funeral."

The Green Maiden couldn't stand the thought of Affey losing her twin sister. The Green Maiden prayed that the Oracle's vision was not of Minda.

"There is something else, Green Maiden. As I sat with the Dar Lantern, a brief, fleeting, vision frequently appeared on the fringes of my sight. If I am correct, the librarian who is the keeper of Sacred Fairy Scrolls at Clonfert House may hold the final key to subdue the Sorcerer Corradhu. How, I do not know."

Mention of the Sacred Fairy Scrolls allayed the Green Maiden's fears, at least for the moment. The Scrolls were safe at Clonfert House. She was sure the Headmaster would be consulting them at this very moment looking for ways to defeat the Sorcerer Corradhu and his curse.

"There is nothing more to tell you, Green Maiden," the Oracle said. "I should return to the Cave of the Dar Lantern."

"Can you wait for Affey to return? It won't be much longer. I'm sure she would want to say goodbye."

"Of course, I will wait. I planned on seeing Affey before I go. I have something to tell her," the Oracle said.

"What," the Green Maiden inquired.

"That is between Affey and me, Green Maiden." The Oracle said nothing more. The Green Maiden was not sure how to respond, so she said nothing.

"Mistress, we are back," Botsam announced from a branch above where the Oracle and the Green Maiden sat. They both stood up as Affey climbed down to meet them.

"How was your adventure with the guardians, Affey," the Green Maiden asked trying her best to sound upbeat.

"A lot of fun just as you said, Green Maiden." Affey was still energized from her time with Botsam and the guardians.

"I'm going to leave that two of you to say goodbye. Oracle, thank you." The Green Maiden bowed to the Oracle. "Come along, Botsam. Tell me about what you showed Affey." Botsam and the Green Maiden disappeared up into the branches.

"Do you have to go so soon?" asked Affey.

"The Cave of the Dar Lantern is where I belong, Affey. Coming here to see you and the Green Maiden was most unusual. Before I go, there is something I must share with you. I expect this will be the first of many things you and I will talk about in the years ahead."

"I hope so, Oracle. I see how the Green Maiden relies on you." Affey paused to consider how to say what she wanted to say next. "I trust I can do the same." Affey spoke almost as if it was a command. Her tone surprised her. Was this the proper way to talk the Oracle of the Dar Lantern? Was this part of her transition into being the eighth Green Maiden? The Oracle didn't seem to take offense.

"I will, I promise you, Affey. I learned something in my contemplations with the Dar Lantern that affects you. The visions weren't very clear. Of this much I am certain. Before this is all over with the Sorcerer Corradhu, you will be severely tested. There will be times when you must insist others follow you. Some of them may not want to follow you. You will have to decide what to do about them if and when that happens. Some of those decisions could be harmful to them should they resist you. Some of those close to you may not survive this confrontation with the Sorcerer Corradhu. In the end, the Western Quarter will be rescued, but only after you have come into your full power as Green Maiden. You must never be deterred, especially when sacrifices have to be made."

Affey stood there trembling. The Oracle's predictions terrified her. Someone, maybe more than one, would die. Could she prevent it? What if the Oracle was wrong and the Sorcerer Corradhu could not be defeated?

"Affey!" The Oracle said sternly. "You will not fail. The Sorcerer Corradhu's curse will be lifted. There is nothing you can do to stop the harm necessary for his defeat."

"Oh Oracle, I'm only a teenager. Why does the world ask these things of me?" Affey was near tears.

"Because you are who you are Affey. You are the first mortal to become a Green Maiden. You are the beginning of a new era. Your future as Green

Maiden is assured. I have had glimpses of your reign and it is wonderful. I have also seen the dangers and obstacles ahead, at least a few of them. You are strong, Affey. You are more powerful than you can imagine. Trust my words. I must go now. You should go the Green Maiden. It is time to prepare to confront the Sorcerer Corradhu. One last thing, Affey. Tonight, while you sleep, you will undergo the final ritual to complete your transformation as the eighth Green Maiden. Tomorrow the end of the Sorcerer Corradhu begins." With those final words, the Oracle vanished leaving Affey alone at the foot of the Eo Mugna Tree.

Chapter 10
Clonfert House New Assignments

The Headmaster stood far enough away from where Kevin was practicing creating the inescapable dome and impenetrable walls so that Kevin could not see him. The Headmaster didn't want Kevin to know he was being watched. It was important that the Headmaster be able to assess what Kevin was capable of before formulating the final plans to confront the Sorcerer Corradhu. From where he stood, it appeared Kevin was having difficulties.

Kevin chose a small clearing in a stand of sycamore trees that was thick with underbrush. Broken branches were scattered everywhere indicating the trees broke under Kevin's power. Sycamores are notorious for shedding large limbs under any kind of stress. The underbrush was a messy tangle. Clearly, Kevin had chosen the wrong place to practice. The Headmaster had to step in. Kevin needed someplace more like the Sorcerer Corradhu's encampment to practice. Where Kevin was practicing was not like it at all. The Headmaster could see Kevin was frustrated. He had to take Kevin to a better location in the eastern forest.

"Kevin," the Headmaster called out as he approached him, "seems the trees are no match for your skill."

Kevin looked around at the mess he made of the clearing. "I picked this spot because sycamores are some of the oldest trees in the world. This stand of appears quite old, so I thought they'd be stronger. I guess I didn't choose well, Headmaster."

"I'm sure your efforts here will prove useful, but we must get you to a proper clearing with proper trees for your practice to be most productive. Time is of the essence. We cannot waste any more time here with these sycamores." The Headmaster started walking deeper into the forest. "Come with me. I have a better spot for you."

Kevin followed the Headmaster and said, "I'm sorry to have wasted time, Headmaster."

"Put that out of your head, Kevin. I have every confidence that where I am taking you will give you enough time and opportunity to hone your Transcendental Movement skills so that we get what we need from you for our plan to drive out the Sorcerer Corradhu."

The Headmaster and Kevin walked another half of a mile into the forest to a large clearing surrounded by an ancient growth of pines. The undergrowth was mature. The Headmaster stopped when he reached the middle of the clearing.

"You will practice here. This is as close to the Sorcerer Corradhu's encampment that we have. You should find the pines and underbrush here more cooperative. I will be back in a few hours to see how you are doing. Remember, time is short. Would you like me to send Professor Mbaye or Smiley to help you?" The Headmaster thought Kevin might like their assistance.

"I'll be fine, Headmaster. If I need their help, I will ask myself." Kevin surveyed the thick growth of pines surrounding the clearing. The underbrush here was more uniform. "I think you are right, Headmaster, this is a much better spot to practice. I had better get started." Kevin turned away from the Headmaster and began.

The Headmaster started back toward Clonfert House, but just before he would be out of sight of Kevin, he looked back to see how Kevin was doing. His was pleased to see that Kevin had already arched the trees over the clearing. He was easily intertwining their branches. Kevin would be ready when it was time to entrap the Sorcerer Corradhu.

As he was about to open the door to his study, the Headmaster distinctly heard two voices. Minda's and the voice of an older woman. It was an unfamiliar voice. He detected a slight trace of an Italian accent. Had one of the Sorcerer Corradhu's witches already infiltrated Clonfert House? The Headmaster thrust open the door ready for a confrontation.

"Headmaster," Minda said rushing over to him. "This is Assunta. She has fled from the Sorcerer Corradhu's encampment. She is one of the Eleven Sisters of the Coven. She wants to help us." Minda motioned for Assunta to approach the Headmaster.

"Headmaster, it is my pleasure to meet you." She wanted the Headmaster to see that she was sincere and not a threat, but the way she spoke and carried herself called her sincerity into question. Assunta was naturally seductive. She couldn't help it. It was her nature to disarm everyone with her charm.

The Headmaster was not charmed. He was on his guard. "You are a witch. Am I correct, Assunta?"

"I am. As your student has informed you, I am one of the Eleven Sister s of the Coven. I am one in a long line of witch sisters. I have come to you because the Sorcerer Corradhu poses an imminent threat not just to the spirit world, but to your world, and our world as well. He must be stopped. I have come here to help you do that." Assunta wasn't sure if the Headmaster believed her or not, but she was sure she had made her commitment to stop the Sorcerer Corradhu clear,

The Headmaster crossed to his desk. He sat in his leather chair. He looked first to Assunta and then to Minda. He was trying to determine if Minda was under a spell form the witch. He didn't say anything at first. He took his time before he spoke.

"Minda," the Headmaster wanted to hear more from her. "Tell me this: from what you have seen do you believe the witch Assunta is telling the truth?" Her answer would reveal if she was under a spell. He didn't ask what, if anything, Minda saw while remote viewing the Sorcerer Corradhu. He didn't want Assunta to know Minda had that skill.

Minda didn't hesitate with her answer. "She is Headmaster. What I saw happening at the Sorcerer Corradhu's encampment was very scary. I can tell you everything now if you like."

"Maybe later." The Headmaster found it curious that Assunta did not ask how Minda knew what she did. "Can you tell me, Minda, what you saw with regard to this witch," the Headmaster asked. He emphasized the word 'saw' to see if the witch Assunta reacted to it. She did not.

"It's more what I didn't see. Of all the Sisters of the Coven, Assunta was the only one who fled from the Western Quarter. At no time did I see her in private conversation with the Sorcerer Corradhu. I remember that when I saw her take off in a different direction than the other sisters, I wondered if she might be coming here. I have seen nothing to indicate she is a spy or any kind of threat." Minda addressed the Headmaster in a way that she had not done before. She spoke to him almost as a colleague rather than his student. When she finished, she was quite proud of herself. She thought Affey would be too. Assunta still did not react to what Minda reported.

The Headmaster invited the witch Assunta to take a seat at his desk. She and Minda sat opposite the Headmaster.

"Very well, Assunta, I trust my student, perhaps more than I should, but I choose to believe her."

Assunta remained quiet and motionless during the Headmaster and Minda's conversation. Now, she had something to say. She was passionate in her words.

"Headmaster. I don't know how this student knows what she does. To me, it doesn't matter. I am just thankful that she saw what she did. It confirms that I am here of my own free will. It confirms I have only the best intentions. Coming here was the most difficult decision I have ever made. The consequences for me and my lineage will be devastating. I am willing to endure this because, if I don't, and if you fail at stopping the Sorcerer Corradhu, he will gain dominion over the forces of the world and all that is good and right will disappear. I cannot be a part of that. I will sacrifice everything to see that he is stopped."

Assunta's words convinced the Headmaster that she was at Clonfert House for all the right reasons.

"Thank you for your candor, Assunta. You may not know this, but I have had an encounter with Corradhu in my past. Our meeting then was unpleasant, to say the least. We do not like each other. Putting that aside, what can you tell me of this curse? Is there an antidote or some counter-curse?" The Headmaster wanted to get to the nature of the curse before he addressed how to deal with the Sorcerer Corradhu.

"I am sorry. Headmaster. I do not. We sisters have been told that there is no remedy for the curse, nor is there any way to repel it. All I know is that the curse must be renewed each day at the same hour. The sorcerer always casts the curse an hour before sunrise. The ritual of the curse can only be performed once a day. If it is not, then the curse ends until the ritual is performed the next day. I am sorry, Headmaster, but that is all I know. I wish I could tell you more." Assunta was truly sorry she didn't have more of an answer.

Minda then started to say, "Headmaster this seems easy enough."

"Not now, Minda." The Headmaster still had reservations about how much to say in front of the witch Assunta.

"Assunta, is there anything else you can tell me that might help," the Headmaster asked.

Assunta thought and thought if there was anything more she could offer. She was searching her memory for anything that might help. The Headmaster and Minda waited.

Two things came to her, though she didn't know if either of them was helpful.

"The Sorcerer Corradhu spends most of his time apart from the Sisters of the Coven in his private encampment somewhere in the forest. None of us witches know where it is. I'm not sure about this next thing. It seems that he depends on his sapphire staff. I have never seen him without it. I think much of his power comes from it. I can't think of anything else, Headmaster. I am sorry I don't have more to offer you." Assunta folded her hands in her lap and looked down at the floor.

"Assunta, what you told me is very useful. Thank you." The Headmaster stood up. "I am going to have Minda take you to a guest room. You are welcome to stay here for as long as you like. For the time being, I must insist you stay with us. I am sure I will have need of you soon enough. Please take our guest to a room to rest," he said to Minda. Assunta was tired. She was also afraid. She offered no resistance.

"Minda," the Headmaster called to her as she was leaving with Assunta, "please return once Assunta is settled. There is something I need you to do."

"I will, Headmaster," Minda replied as she closed his study door behind her.

The Headmaster was about to go to visit Professor O'Riley and Michael in the secret library when there was a small noise at his door. It sounded like a bird pecking on the oak door.

"Yes," he called out, "who is it?"

There was no answer, only another peck. The Headmaster went and opened the door. At first, he didn't see anyone. As he turned to close the door, a voice came from the floor below him. There stood the tiniest fairy the Headmaster had ever seen. She was the color of a pink rose. Her wings were tipped in silver.

"I'm so sorry madam. I almost stepped on you."

The beautiful, tiny fair flew up before his face. She may be tiny, but she was feisty. She was a bold fairy. She had an errand to complete and she had no time to chit-chat.

"The Oracle of the Dar Lantern, my mistress, sent me to you with an urgent message," the fairy said with the most serious expression on her face. She flew into the Headmaster's study and landed on his desk, her hands on her hips. She was in a hurry to deliver her message. The Headmaster followed her after closing the study door.

"What is the message you are so anxious to deliver?"

"She told me to tell you to find the volume marked '962' in the Secret Library. It will lead you to something you need to know to repel the Sorcerer Corradhu. That is the entire message I have to deliver – all of it." Having delivered the message from the Oracle, the fairy started toward the Headmaster's study door. She was too small to open it.

"Do you mind, Headmaster? I must get back to the Cave of the Dar Lantern. It's getting late and I don't like being alone in the dark."

The Headmaster hesitated before opening the door. "Is that all there is? Nothing else," he asked the fairy.

She responded curtly, "if there was something else, I would have told you. What do you take me for, a fool? You mortals! Open the door. Please?" The Headmaster opened his study door and watched as the tiny, feisty, bold fairy flew off down the corridor and around a corner.

Even though the Headmaster wanted to go immediately to the Secret Library to tell Professor O'Riley and Michael what the fairy said, he returned to his desk. In a locked drawer he kept a handwritten journal entitled, "Items of Special Interest for Headmasters in the Secret Library." It was the one and only manuscript reserved solely for Headmasters. No one else knew about. It was passed down from Headmaster to Headmaster. The very existence of the journal was the most secret of all the Clonfert House's secrets.

The Headmaster unlocked the drawer of his desk where it was kept. He unfastened the clasp that secured the binding. He quickly skimmed through its contents until he found the entry for the year '962'. Certain volumes in the Secret Library were identified by the year that they were assembled. There was a brief notation in volume 962 that read: The Su Nuraxi Problem. That was the entire entry. There was no comment, no explanation, no cross-reference. *How odd*, thought the Headmaster. He closed the clasp on the book, locked it, and placed it back in the desk drawer. He locked the drawer and put the key back in his pocket.

The Headmaster sat back in his chair. What happened in 962? What did the Su Nuraxi have to do with it? Was history repeating itself? How did the Oracle of the Dar Lantern know about volume 962? He had never heard any mention of it in all his years at Clonfert House. Of course, there was much about the Secret Library that was unknown. What is in this volume 962? The Headmaster had to go to the Secret Library and find out. Just as he opened his study door to leave, Minda returned.

"Where are you going Headmaster," Minda asked. She noticed he seemed distracted and in a hurry.

"I will be back shortly. Minda, please reconnect your view to the Sorcerer Corradhu. See if you can pinpoint his private encampment. It is near the ritual grounds, as you heard Assunta tell us. Make note of where he keeps his sapphire staff." The Headmaster walked quickly down the corridor.

Minda sat down at the table in the Headmaster's study. She quickly re-established Remote Viewing the Sorcerer Corradhu's ritual clearing. She swept her vision wide and found the Sorcerer Corradhu's private encampment. She didn't like what she saw.

The Sorcerer Corradhu's private encampment was guarded by creatures that looked like a cross between a bird and a serpent. These creatures were quite large. The intensity of their vigilance was like nothing Minda had ever seen. Yet, they looked familiar. Where had she seen creatures like this before? Was it at Master Chan Wu's house? No, those were Fu Dogs. Where had she seen them? "A temple, some kind of temple, that's where I've seen them," she said aloud.

She figured out what they were. "They are nagas," she said as if someone was waiting for her to name them. Nagas are mythological creatures guarding Hindu and Buddhist temples in Asia. What were they doing guarding the Sorcerer Corradhu? They were no myth.

From her more recent studies, she knew that their mythology says that nagas are guardians of the earth's treasures. They are quick to anger and violence, especially with anyone who endangers the earth. They highly value purity of mind, body, and intention. How could such creatures be in service to the Sorcerer Corradhu? What had happened to them to make them forsake their nature? If they had fallen under some spell of the Sorcerer Corradhu, then he really was a most powerful sorcerer. One thing was certain, getting past the nagas to capture the Sorcerer Corradhu would be very difficult and dangerous. Perhaps even deadly. She has to tell the Headmaster about them NOW!

Chapter 11

The Eo Mugna Tree Affey's Initiation as the Eighth Green Maiden

It had been a long morning for Affey. Her transformation to the eighth Green Maiden began. The Oracle of the Dar Lantern shared her dark visions. Affey spent an hour with Botsam and the other guardians romping through the forest. Now, she was alone under the Eo Mugna tree. She was tired. All Affey wanted to do was lay down under the tree's green canopy and take a nap.

The Green Maiden was watching Affey from high up in the branches. She knew, because couple of the Oracle told her, that Affey's initiation as Green Maiden would happen the next time Affey fell asleep. The Green Maiden had to be vigilant so that she would not miss the precise moment that she must give Affey the special sleeping potion that would ensure the initiation dream. Affey must experience the same dream all Green Maiden's did during their final physical transformation. The Green Maiden had not planned on Affey's initiation for a least another few years. She wondered if Affey's initiation dream would to be different. Affey was no spirit girl becoming a Green Maiden. She was a mortal and the Green Maiden had no idea what Affey's dream would be like. Maybe she wouldn't have a dream at all. Although she had reservations about giving Affey the special sleeping potion, it had to be done and done now. She sent Botsam down to Affey with the potion.

"Hello, Botsam," Affey said eyeing the cup in his hand. "Having a drink, are you?"

"No, miss, this is for you. The Green Maiden thought it might refresh you." Botsam handed her the cup with the potion. He didn't mention anything about what was about to happen. The Oracle already prepared Affey for this moment.

"Tell her I said, 'thank you', Botsam. I am tired after all that has happened today. I think I'll rest here under the Eo Mugna Tree for a while." Affey took the cup and drank it all down in a single gulp. "This is delicious, Botsam." She handed the cup back to Botsam then laid down under the Eo Mugna Tree.

"I'll keep an eye on you, miss. If you fall asleep, I'll wake you in time for dinner,"

"I would appreciate that very much, Botsam."

Botsam climbed up a few branches above Affey where he stayed keeping watch over her.

It didn't take long for the potion to take effect. Affey drifted into a tranquil sleep. Her breath came slow and steady. The dream began. Nothing was on display. All she saw was a soft, white glow. Affey wasn't sure how long she remained with the white glow before she heard faint voices. They were coming from the distant horizon of her dream. She cocked her head as if this would make it easier to understand the voices. They were female. She was sure about that. They were getting closer. They must be the visitors the Oracle predicted. One by one they emerged from the foggy, white glow.

There were five of them. Each was dressed in a separate color. They were of various ages, height, weight, complexion, and eye color. Yet, Affey detected some vague quality that suggested they were somehow related. The oldest one, the one dressed all in black, spoke to Affey first.

"Hello, Affey. We are the Green Maiden's Spirit Sisters. We are here to witness your initiation as the eighth Green Maiden. We always witness this most auspicious event." Their presence comforted Affey.

Under the spell of the potion Botsam brought her, she was fully awake within the dream. She asked the sister dressed in black, "What have you come to do to?"

"We are simply here to witness your initiation as the eighth Green Maiden," the Orange Sister said.

The blue sister stepped up next and told Affey, "Your final transformation requires you to be initiated into the sisterhood. We are here to watch and welcome you. The ritual will be performed by of all of the previous Green Maidens who are about to arrive."

No sooner had the blue sister spoken than the six previous Green Maidens, all of whom past on eons ago, approached from the edge of Affey's dream. Affey noticed that the current Green Maiden was not with them. It must be because she was still alive. Affey felt as if she lost touch with her body. She didn't know if she was still sitting under the Eo Mugna Tree, laying down, or standing up. The ground beneath her was invisible. Was she floating? It was disorienting. Once the Green Maidens were close to Affey one of them spoke.

"Affey Temne, daughter of Wilfred and Johnathan Temne, we are here this beautiful day to…" The Green Maiden abruptly stopped speaking. She and the other Green Maidens turned around suddenly to look into the distance. Affey also looked. Then she heard it.

At first, Affey wasn't sure what she heard, but then it became louder. It was the sound of trumpets, cymbals, and drums. She looked to the Green Maidens and the Spirit Sisters for some explanation, but they were fixed on the direction the sound was coming from. One by one, the Green Maidens and Spirit Sisters fell to their knees and touched their foreheads to the invisible ground. Whoever was coming was unexpected. Whoever it was, inspired awe in the Green Maidens and Spirit Sisters.

Affey remained standing. She couldn't take her eyes off the place from where the sound of the cymbals, drums, and trumpets emanated. Then, out of the mist of the white glow, a banner appeared. It fluttered, suspended in the air. No one was holding it aloft. Across the banner was a splash of color and several glyphs. Affey did a quick translation in her head. The glyphs said: The Twenty-Two Celestial Sirens. Emerging under the banner to the sound of the trumpets, cymbals, and drums, were two columns of eleven women moving solemnly toward Affey. The Green Maidens and Spirit Sisters remained kneeling on the invisible ground. As the women drew closer, Affey saw that they were identical in very way. The Sirens were each dressed in a flowing, purple gown. Their auburn hair was tied with a silver band into a braid that fell almost to the ground behind them. Their skin was almost as white as the glow that engulphed the dream. They were all barefoot. They moved as one with beauty and grace.

Affey studied about the Twenty-Two Celestial Sirens at Saint Brendan's Academy. She learned that they dwelled in a realm apart from all other realms. There, they were responsible for the movement of the planets, moons, stars, everything in the heavens. They were immortal. Their realm was a multi-universe beyond time, space, and thought. How they did what they did was beyond one's ability to comprehend. In fact, she had been taught that the Twenty-Two Celestial Sirens were more of a metaphor than an actuality. *Apparently,* she thought, *what I have learned about them is wrong. They were real and they were here in her dream.* Affey didn't know what she should do.

Should she kneel as the Green Maidens and Spirit Sisters did? She couldn't make up her mind so stood as still as she could.

As they got closer, Affey picked up the distinct fragrance of jasmine. Affey took notice that she was becoming completely relaxed. It felt as if this was exactly what should be happening to her. She looked at her hands. They were no longer pale green. They were as deep an emerald green as the rarest jade. She was as green as the most verdant forest. A tear slipped from her eyes.

The Twenty-Two celestial Sirens made a circle around Affey. The Green Maidens and the Spirit Sisters stood up and circled behind them. All of them, the Green Maidens, the Spirit Sisters, the Twenty-Two Celestial Sirens, were looking at Affey with more affection than she had ever experienced, even from her own mother or father. Two of the Sirens broke out from the circle and approached Affey.

Neither one of them spoke, yet Affey understood what was coming next. Affey held her arms out to her sides. She closed her eyes. She felt her dress being removed and a new one draped over her. The two women lowered Affey's arms. Affey somehow knew it was not yet time for her to open her eyes.

She sensed several of the Sirens were behind her. Without knowing why, she fell back into their waiting arms. They caught her and carried her a short distance. They laid her down on something cold and hard. All Affey could think of was that she was on some sort of altar. Another Siren removed Affey's shoes. Someone, maybe the same siren, bathed her feet.

Next, Affey could feel that she was surrounded by some, but not all, of the sirens. They placed their hands on her. Affey counted twenty-two hands which meant eleven of them were around her. The Sirens started to chant. It was the most beautiful chant Affey ever heard, even though she couldn't understand a single word. As the sirens chanted, Affey felt an energy flow through her. She was convinced that the sirens were summoning the powerful potential she had been feeling recently. Now though, it was no longer a potential. It was power. What kind and for what purpose she would have to wait and experience, but this was power. A real, immediate, physical power. It swept through her with such force that Affey thought she would burst into flames. Then, just as suddenly as it had started, it stopped. The twenty-two hands were lifted from her body. Affey still didn't think it was time to open her eyes.

Another one of The Twenty-Two Celestial sirens stood just above and behind Affey's head. This siren placed her hands on either side of Affey's face. Her touch was cool and comforting. Affey could have stayed there forever the siren's touch was so soothing. The Siren spoke.

"Affey Temne, Daughter of the Universe, Sister of the Earth, Air, Water, Fire, and Space, Empress of the Wind and the Woods. You are the one of whom the prophecy said:

"There will be seven, in the old way.
The eighth begins anew.
She will rise up in the north
In a house of scholarship and secret.
Her emerald essence awakens swiftly.
Here birth nature cast off."

The Siren continued. "You are the one from the north from just such a house, Clonfert House. It is up to you to restore balance and harmony wherever you see discord or disaster. You will have allies. You will have help. But, Affey Temne, Daughter of the Universe, Sister of the Earth, Air, Water, Fire, and Space, Empress of the Wind and the Woods, take heed of the rest of the prophecy which says:

Beware the Dark Magician.
Triumph makes war with tragedy."

The Siren holding Affey's head felt Affey tense up with anxiety when hearing the ominous words of the prophecy. She then told Affey.

"There is one final part of the prophecy and it says:

The emerald empress prevails
All worlds orbit as one."

Affey released some, but not all, of her anxiety. The siren removed her hands from Affey's face and stepped away. Affey still wasn't ready to open her eyes, but another one of The Twenty-Two Celestial Sirens called out Affey's name. It commanded her to sit up and open her eyes.

Affey followed the Siren's command and stood up at the foot of the altar. In turn, each of the prior Green Maidens and the Spirit Sisters came up to Affey, kissed her on both cheeks, and touched their forehead to hers. When the last of them performed this part of the ceremony, all the women were in a single circle surrounding Affey. She looked to each of them as if to say both thank you and please be of help to me. The part of the circle of women that was directly in front of Affey parted. Her mother and father were standing there. Affey wanted to rush to them, to embrace them, but she held back. She was the new Green Maiden.

Affey didn't know what to expect from her parent's presence. Yes, they were enchanters just as she was. Her parents were renowned experts in their respective fields of skill and power. They must know what this means for them. Their daughter will outlive them by centuries. They may never see her again. Was this a good-bye?

"My dear daughter," Affey's mother said, "we are so proud of you. To think, our daughter, a mortal, is a Green Maiden. How fortunate the world is to have you." Her mother was crying softly.

"Affey," her father said as he walked toward her, "we know that this means you will be far from us in many ways. We are enchanters. We are heirs to the Clonfert Compact. Your destiny is all of our destiny."

Her mother joined her father. They took Affey's hands in theirs. "As of this moment you are the Green Maiden. You are still our daughter and always will be. Though you live now in the spirit realm, you can come to us whenever you choose," Affey's mother said.

"Keep watch over Minda," her father asked.

"Minda is always in my thoughts. We are sisters still," Affey said to reassure her parents.

"And you will forever be my mother and father." She kissed them both. Together, her parents walked back into the white glow of her dream and disappeared.

All the women, Sirens, Spirit Sisters, Green Maidens, reformed the circle around Affey. With one voice they said, "Affey Temne, daughter of the universe, sister of earth, air, water, fire, and space, empress of the wind and the woods, you are the eighth Green Maiden, not just in this moment, not for the next five hundred years, but forever, even in death."

A clap of thunder rolled through Affey's dream. A single bolt of lightning blinded her. When her eyes cleared, she was alone. The white glow of her dream had turned a faint shade of green. She heard her name called.

"Green Maiden. Green Maiden. Wake up. It's time for supper." It was Botsam calling her name.

Affey, the eighth Green Maiden, woke from her dream. She was sitting up against the trunk of the Eo Mugna Tree. She looked down. She was dressed as the Green Maiden. Her skin was emerald green. If only she had a mirror.

"Botsam. What color is my hair," she asked him.

"What color should it be?" Botsam asked. He smiled at her then said, with a slight, formal bow, "Green Maiden."

Chapter 12
Clonfert House The Secret Library

Michael stood in awe of the Secret Library. Not only were some of the world's rarest and most important documents housed here, but the entirety of spirit lore and legend was documented in the vast array of volumes, manuscripts, and odd bits of paper. The Secret Library was enormous. The roof was so high that light barely reached the beams and rafters. Michael guessed that there must be hundreds of miles of shelves alone. He did not know how to gage the number of chests, cabinets, file drawers, and miscellaneous pieces of furniture that were scattered everywhere. There was also the modern digital library that resided on a server so large that it occupied its own wing of the Secret Library. Michael couldn't see where the library ended. This made sense to him since all the wisdom of all worlds, spirit, animal, and human was contained in the Secret Library. Name a realm, and all its knowledge, teachings, and secrets could be found somewhere in the Secret Library. *How remarkable*, Michael thought to himself, *that this world of wisdom exists behind a plain oak door simply marked, "Library."*

Once they entered the Secret Library, Professor O'Riley took Michael to a room immediately to the left of the entrance door. On a brass placard above the arch leading to the room were the words, "Chart Room." This room alone, Michael estimated, was the size of a soccer field. The walls were lined with map cases and chart tables. Arranged neatly down the center of the room, in a single line, large oaken tables were setup for use. They were clear except for a lamp and writing pad. Globes of various sizes and vintage could be found in the nooks and crannies. Telescopes seemed set to peer into the sky, even though there was not a single window in the Secret Library. Navigational devices such as astrolabes, sextants, and compasses were gathered in groupings as if they were being prepared to be boxed up for shipment to some foreign land, Michael also saw weird, unusual devices whose use he couldn't even begin to guess. Professor O'Riley led them to a table in the middle of the room.

"Michael," Professor O'Riley began, "as you can tell, the Secret Library is formidable. It is impossible to know its contents. That is why this, the 'Chart Room', exists. While it is a legitimate chart room, it also serves as the locus of the inventory of every, single thing housed here in this Secret Library. The only thing not here is the Secret Fairy Scrolls. For now, at least, there are located someplace safe." Professor O'Riley wasn't exactly being truthful with Michael. They were in the Secret Library, though hidden within it even further. He didn't want Michael distracted by wanting to see them again. Professor O'Riley turned Michael's attention back to the reason why they were in the Secret Library.

"We must get to work on locating any information we can about the Sorcerer Corradhu's curse."

"How, Professor? The inventory or catalogue of the library's contents itself must be unwieldy. Where do we start?" Michael thought they had been given an impossible assignment by the Headmaster.

"Michael, even though there are countless books, texts, manuscripts, maps, charts, indices, correspondence, etc. here, everything has been cataloged and uploaded onto the Secret Library's server. All you must do is search the database. Use that computer terminal over there," Professor O'Riley said indicating a terminal on a nearby wall. "It's like a google search. Type in keyword words and a list of all relevant materials will be displayed."

"Sounds simple enough," Michael said. "What terms do we search first?"

Professor O'Riley handed Michael a piece of paper with an initial list of terms for Michael to start searching. However, before he began, Michael had a question.

"Professor O'Riley, I have to ask you something. I'm thinking that you don't maintain the Secret Library or this database by yourself. Who helps you?"

"An astute question, Michael." Professor O'Riley hadn't expected Michael to ask this question so soon, but as the Professor's successor as librarian of Clonfert House, he might as well explain to Michael how the Secret Library is maintained.

"The answer to your question requires I reveal the most secret, secret of the Secret Library. First, I don't maintain anything in this library at all. There is a special, mostly anonymous, tribe of spirits, who are the masters of the Secret Library. They do everything. They catalogue new arrivals, preserve all the texts, volumes, manuscripts, devices, maps, charts, and so on. They also maintain the database. How they do what they do remains a mystery, even to me. Yet, they are meticulous in their work."

"Are they here now," Michael asked.

"I'm afraid that is yet another secret. I have only ever met their supervisor once, when he paid me a visit to introduce himself. It was shortly after I took over as the librarian of Clonfert House. Since that one time, I have not seen him again nor have I ever seen a single member of his tribe. When I am here, though, I can sense their presence. I know they are watching. I can feel it. Someday you will too, Michael." This raised another question for Michael.

"How often to you come here to the Secret Library, Professor? How about other professors or students?"

"Not often. Only the Headmaster and I have authority to be in the Secret Library. Students are absolutely forbidden to enter. The fact that you are here now is an exception to the rules. Now, back to work."

Michael took a quick look into the shadows and corners looking for any sign the spirits were about. Nothing. He turned to the list of key words given to him by Professor O'Riley. Meanwhile, Professor O'Riley sat working on a list of more search terms.

The first terms Michael searched were: sorcerer, Corradhu. The computer terminal displayed a list of 1,801 entries related to the combination of the two words. Michael sent the list to the printer. Then Michael searched 'stregheria'. 63,954 entries were listed. There were too many items listed to be useful. Then he typed in 'Su Nuraxi'. Curiously, only two entries were displayed. However, there was a comment added at the bottom of the list that read, "narrow your search." Again, a curiosity. Michael typed in the only word he could think of that might narrow the search: curse. He slowly typed in the word: c...u...r...s...e...The search wheel on the cursor started spinning. The database wasn't responding as fast as it did for the other searches. Michael was about to call Professor O'Riley to look at the screen when the Headmaster burst through the Secret Library door and charged into the Chart Room.

"Stop what you are doing," the Headmaster shouted almost out of breath.

Michael looked to Professor O'Riley for some direction as to what he should do. Professor O'Riley mimed 'stop typing'.

The Headmaster was standing over Michael's shoulder now. Professor O'Riley joined him.

"Type in 'volume 962'," the Headmaster said to Michael. Michael typed in the search term as fast as he could. The cursor wheel stopped spinning and displayed: 962-Year of the Su Nuraxi Problem. Room 97, stack 338, shelf 2. The Headmaster instructed Professor O'Riley take Michael to retrieve the volume and bring it back.

"You two go and fetch the volume. We must examine it immediately."

"That won't be necessary." A refined, rich voice carried down from the rafters high above where the three of them stood. They looked up.

A barely visible wisp of vapor was floating down toward them. When it was in front of them, the most wonderful creature materialized in the air. Professor O'Riley whispered to Michael, "it's the supervisor."

"I assume he probably figured that out O'Riley, judging from your prior mention of me to this child." The Supervisor said the world 'child' as if the word turned sour in his mouth.

So, Michael thought, *they were listening and watching.*

The creature moved slightly so that he was face-to-face with Michael. "You best remember that, boy." Again, he emphasized the word 'boy'.

The creature speaking to Michael was about three feet tall. Michael would later describe him to Kevin and Minda as 'distinguished'. The spirit had very human features. His neatly trimmed hair was silver as was his beard. He was dressed in a navy blue, three-piece suit with chalk pinstripes. His shirt was brilliantly white. Around his neck he wore a silver bow tie that matched the color of his hair and beard. A silver watch fob draped across the front of vest on which hung a ring of bejeweled keys. A silver monocle dangled from the chest pocket on his suit jacket. His brown shoes were shined to a high brilliance. Michael though of the phrase, 'a gentleman and a scholar'.

To Michaels chagrin, the Supervisor said, "I am both, Michael. I am a gentleman and a scholar."

Michael also though the Supervisor was a little full of himself.

The Headmaster was anxious to understand what the Supervisor meant when he said it 'would not be necessary' to locate volume 962.

"Boru," the Supervisor said using the Headmasters first name, "let's all take a seat and I'll explain."

"Master Bromley," the Headmaster said.

So that's his name, Michael noted. Mater Bromley, the Supervisor, nodded to Michael to show, again, he knew what Michael was thinking.

"Master Bromley, please," the Headmaster implored the Supervisor. "What is the meaning of this? Why is it unnecessary for us to fetch volume 962?"

"Two reasons, Headmaster. First, you are not authorized to see it. Neither are you O'Riley. And certainly, you don't think this child would be permitted to see it," Master Bromley said pointing at Michael.

"And why is that, Master Bromley?" The Headmaster was angry. Michael had never seen the Headmaster angry. Professor O'Riley tugged at the Headmaster's sleeve, but the Headmaster yanked it away. "You are overstepping your authority, Master Bromley."

"We shall see, Boru, we shall see." Master Bromley was not the least bit phased by the Headmaster's anger. "More importantly, Boru, it is of no use to you."

Again, the Headmaster, asked, "why, Master Bromley? In your infinite wisdom, you must know why we need it." The Headmaster's sarcasm was not lost on Master Bromley.

"What you need, Boru, is to calm down. I will help you, but perhaps not in the way you wish."

Master Bromley indicated they should all take a seat at the table. Once they were seated Master Bromley said, "you want to defeat the Sorcerer Corradhu. Yes, I've been following these events."

"Then you know how dire things are becoming, Master Bromley," Professor O'Riley said.

"Yes, Professor, I do. And that is why I am sitting here with you now." Master Bromley reached into the inside his vest pocket to look at his watch. He glanced at it for a second then placed it back. He plucked the monocle and polished it with a handkerchief. "The truth, Headmaster, Professor," addressing them both more formally, "is that volume 962 went missing sometime in 1738. We have been unable to recover it, but given the Sorcerer Corradhu's actions, either he has it in his possession, or he gained knowledge of its contents. Fortunately, I too know the entire contents of volume 962."

Michael spoke up, "then you can share it with us."

The look the Headmaster gave Michael was withering. It was as if he had slapped Michael.

"Apologies, Headmaster," Michael said on the verge of tears.

"Well, Master Bromley," the Headmaster said, "will you share what you know with us?"

"No, I will not, Headmaster. It cannot fall into mortal's hands." The Headmaster was about to challenge him. Master Bromley quickly shut him down. "Stop, Headmaster, before you let your anger get the best of you. I can give you some guidance that will help you. Please stop interrupting me. I have other things to attend to and you are wasting my time with your questions."

"Please, Master Bromley, tell us," Professor O'Riley said, hoping to ease the growing tension between the Headmaster and Master Bromley.

"The first thing you must accept is that the Sorcerer Corradhu cannot be defeated, but his curse can be lifted. Any effort made to defeat him will be fruitless. As for the curse, you already know that to lift it, you must interrupt its being cast in the first place. This is not an easy thing to accomplish, but it can be done."

The Headmaster had calmed down a little. He asked Master Bromley, "how?"

"The key is to isolate the Sorcerer Corradhu from the Eleven Sisters of the Coven. You must also eliminate the nagas that are his personal guardians. Somehow, you must take from him either the Sacred Soil from the Su Nuraxi or his sapphire staff. They are two of the most powerful elements necessary for the ritual of the curse to be completed. The curse simply cannot be cast without them. Eliminating the nagas is the easier to accomplish, but still quite a challenge. They are ferocious and unpredictable. Nagas has an uncanny ability to anticipate what their opponents will do. There is one, sure way to kill them."

The Headmaster had not heard most of what Master Bromley said. When he mentioned the Sisters of the Coven, he had leaned over to say something to Professor O'Riley. Fortunately, Michael heard it all. Neither one of them heard Michael's question. They should have paid more attention.

"At least one of you has sense enough to ask that important question," Master Bromley said with an obvious slight to the Headmaster and Professor O'Riley who still didn't hear him.

Master Bromley addressed Michael directly as if what he said next only Michael would understand. "Sever their tails. Their tails are lethal weapons. Sever the tail and the Naga dies instantly. Remember this. These two don't seem to be paying attention."

Michael nodded that he understood. The Headmaster did hear Master Bromley again mentioning of the nagas.

"Nagas? In the Western Quarter? You must be mistaken, Master Bromley," the Headmaster said. There was alarm in his voice.

"No, Boru, I am not mistaken. I never am. As you will soon discover, your student, Minda, has seen them. She can tell you more about them. She seems an accomplished student. Smarter than you at that age. Let's move on to the Eleven Sisters of the Coven. Separating the Sorcerer Corradhu from the Eleven Sisters of the Coven is a tough challenge. They are loyal and dedicated to him. Don't let the defector, Assunta, lead you to think others will follow. They will not. They are powerful witches. I venture to say that they would gladly die in defending him. He, however, would not come to their aid if the situation were reversed."

Professor O'Riley asked. "Since you know the abilities of the enchanters here at Clonfert House, can any of them take on the Eleven Sisters of the Coven?"

Michael sighed aloud thinking, "here we go again." Then he recalled that Master Bromley knew what he was thinking. However, Master Bromley didn't react this time.

"Some can and some cannot, Professor. You will have to figure that out. What the Sorcerer Corradhu doesn't know is that he needs at least three Sisters of the Coven to be present when he casts the curse. He thinks they are just adornments to the ritual. The Sorcerer Corradhu believes he can cast the curse by himself. He doesn't know that he cannot cast it without them. He also doesn't know that even his own powers depend on their presence to have full effect, which is why they must be captured first. Or, unfortunately, perhaps killed."

The Headmaster wanted to return to defeating the Sorcerer Corradhu.

"Is there no way to defeat Corradhu? Surely, there must be. No creature is invincible."

"You are correct Headmaster. But there is a difference between defeat and death. Defeat him by lifting the curse. Death will find him in due course."

"Anything else you wish to share, Master Bromley," Professor O'Riley asked.

"There is one more thing I have to say. To take the Sacred Soil and the sapphire staff, the Sorcerer Corradhu must be at his most vulnerable. There is only one who knows when he has reached this point. Only one can stop him. Do not forget that you must only interrupt the curse for one day. It is only then that the Sorcerer Corradhu will understand that he has lost the ability to cast the curse." Master Bromley checked his pocket watch again. "I must be going. You have much to do."

"Who is one you speak of, Master Bromley," Professor O'Riley asked.

Master Bromley, Supervisor of the spirit tribe of the Secret Library at Clonfert House, began to float back up to the rafters. Before he vanished into a vapor he said, "Ask the Green Maiden." He vanished. This would not be the only time Michael would encounter Master Bromley. Neither the Headmaster nor Professor O'Riley would ever see Master Bromley again.

Chapter 13
Clonfert House, The Headmaster's Study Minda's Discoveries

Despite not having found volume 962, the Headmaster and Professor O'Riley were encouraged by Master Bromley's guidance on how to defeat the Sorcerer Corradhu. For his part, Michael, ever the skeptic, thought it was convenient that Master Bromley said volume 962 had gone missing since 1798. Michael didn't believe Master Bromley. What was in volume 962 that required Master Bromley to fabricate the story of a missing volume, especially volume 962? *Maybe,* Michael thought, *I'm wrong. Still,* he wondered, *of the millions of documents housed in the Secret Library, why was only volume 962 missing?* Michael said to himself, "I need to stop thinking like this. What good will it do? Still, someday I hope to find out." Unfortunately, Michael would not find out the truth for a very, very long time.

The Headmaster, Professor O'Riley, and Michael headed up the marble steps that lead from the Secret Library to the Headmaster's study. Each of them was lost in their own thoughts. The Headmaster was thinking of ways to attack the Sorcerer Corradhu and steal the ritual items described by Master Bromley. Professor O'Riley was considering a visit to the Sacred Fairy Scrolls to see what help they might provide. Michael was anxious to know what Minda had discovered during her Remote Viewing of the Sorcerer Corradhu's private encampment. He was about to find out.

Minda was rushing from the Headmaster's study to the Secret Library. As she descended the same staircase the other three were ascending, she intercepted them. Almost out of breath from running as fast as she could. She said, "Headmaster, I have seen something disturbing at the Sorcerer Corradhu's private encampment. I though you should know right away."

"What is it," Michael asked.

"Minda, sit down on the steps for a minute and catch your breath," the Headmaster said trying to calm her.

Minda refused. "Headmaster, I cannot sit down. We must get back to your study so I can keep watch on the Sorcerer Corradhu. I'll explain what I saw on our way back." Minda started to quickly climb the marble steps. It took the other three a few steps to catch up to her.

Minda said, as they climbed the stairs, "The Sorcerer Corradhu's private encampment is guarded by two nagas. Do you know about nagas?" she asked over her shoulder.

"We do," Professor O'Riley replied.

Minda stopped as she reached the top step and snapped around.

"How," she asked. "How could you possibly know when I just discovered them?"

"We will explain later, Minda. We need to get back to my study and you need to re-connect to the Sorcerer Corradhu," the Headmaster said as he stepped past Minda and led the way back to his study. Minda waited for him and Professor O'Riley to move ahead of her. As Michael started to follow them, she grabbed his arm to hold him back.

"What happened in the Secret Library? You have to tell me, Michael."

Michael wasn't sure if he was supposed to keep what happened a secret, but he whispered to Minda, "A Master Bromley, the fairy who supervises the Secret Library, visited us. He knows about the Sorcerer Corradhu and the nagas." That is all he felt he should share with Minda for now.

They reached the Headmaster's study.

Professor O'Riley instructed Michael, "please go back to my study and make a complete record of the events that just transpired in the Secret Library. Make sure that you include each and every detail. Leave nothing out. It is important that we have a record. Do you understand?"

"I do, Professor," Michael said.

Michael returned to Professor O'Riley's study and spent the rest of the day writing and re-writing a statement of the events in the Secret Library. When he was finished, Michael was confident that her had recorded an accurate, detailed, facts-only account of the events. Even though he wanted to record his own view of the events, particularly his misgivings about the 'missing' volume 962, he decided to record them in his personal diary. Many, many years later

Michael's statement of the events and the entries in his diary would re-surface in a time of turmoil and strife.

Back in the Headmaster's study, the Headmaster and Professor O'Riley stood by while Minda reconnected her Remote Viewing to the Sorcerer Corradhu's private encampment.

The Headmaster asked Minda, "can you locate his staff? It is made entirely of sapphires. We believe he keeps it with him at all times, since it possesses its own power. Even so, we wonder if he sets it aside when he is at his private encampment. See if you can locate it."

"Let me try," Minda said.

Minda slowly and methodically scanned the Sorcerer Corradhu's private encampment. She didn't see the Sorcerer anywhere. She was repeatedly distracted by the snarling nagas straining at the chains that tethered them to two large granite pillars in a small clearing in front of the Sorcerer Corradhu's tent. For just a second, she was convinced one of the nagas was staring through her Remote Viewing directly at her. *That isn't possible*, she thought. *Nagas don't have such powers.* She re-focused on locating the Sorcerer Corradhu.

He wasn't anywhere near the nagas. When Minda peered inside his tent he wasn't there either. When she turned her Remote Viewing to the edge of the forest surrounding his private encampment, she found him. The Sorcerer Corradhu was sitting on a moss-covered stump. His eyes were closed as if he were sleeping or in a state of deep contemplation. Minda focused all her intensity on his face. She drew her vision closer and closer. When only his face occupied her entire field of Remote Viewing, the Sorcerer Corradhu opened his eyes and stared straight at her. At least, that is what she thought. Unlike the nagas, the Sorcerer Corradhu was a powerful sorcerer. Remote Viewing was certainly within the realm of possible powers he might possess. Being Minda, though, she was not about to be intimidated by him. She focused on him with all the intensity she could muster. The Sorcerer Corradhu blinked and rubbed his eyes. He wasn't looking at her at all. He was just waking up from a short nap on the mossy stump. Minda was relieved. She reported all of this to the Headmaster and Professor O'Riley as it was happening.

"Do you see his sapphire staff," the Headmaster asked.

"Not yet, but I will," Minda said confidently.

Minda swept her vision over where the Sorcerer Corradhu was sitting. She didn't see the sapphire staff. "It's not with him," she reported.

"Keep looking. It must be there somewhere," Professor O'Riley directed.

Minda withdrew her vision from the Sorcerer Corradhu to focus back on his private encampment. The sapphire staff was there, but it was in a place that would not be easy to approach. "How had I not seen it before? How could I have missed it," she said.

"Where is it," the Headmaster asked.

"Not in a good place," Minda said quietly.

"What do you mean, Minda," the Headmaster asked.

"It is embedded in a good-sized block of granite between the two nagas. About two-thirds of it are embedded in the block. The hilt of the sapphire staff is sticking out of the top, ready to be plucked out. Reminds me of the Sword in the Stone from the King Arthur legend. Grabbing it will be nearly impossible, though, I'm afraid," she volunteered.

"How so?" asked Professor O'Riley.

"Get anywhere near the sapphire staff and the nagas will attack you. They are chained where they are to protect it." Minda could only imagine how terrible an attack by the nagas would be.

"Master Bromley was right about the nagas," the Headmaster said. "Seizing the sapphire staff will be dangerous. It will require special skills and talent." If the Headmaster and Professor O'Riley had paid attention to Master Bromley, they would have heard his comment to Michael about severing the nagas' tails.

Minda didn't respond at all to the mention of Master Bromley. She didn't want to betray Michael's confidence. She didn't say anything about attacking the nagas since she held the opinion that they could not be subdued.

Next, the Headmaster instructed Minda to search for the Sacred Soil of the Su Nuraxi.

"Minda, I am now going to ask you to locate something for us. I am not exactly sure what it looks like or where you should look. I'm hoping your enchanter powers will lead you to it."

"Tell me what it is Headmaster. I will do my best." If anything, Minda was very confident in her enchanting abilities. She would find it, whatever it was.

Professor O'Riley explained. "The Sorcerer Corradhu possesses some of the Sacred Soil of the Su Nuraxi. It is an essential element for the casting of the curse. We have been told that he keeps it with him at all times. Of course, we were told the same thing about his sapphire staff."

"I'll find it. Don't worry. If its soil he carries, then it must be in a pouch of some kind." Minda re-focused her Remote Viewing back toward the Sorcerer Corradhu. She found him walking back to his private encampment.

"He has a leather pouch dangling from his crystal belt," Minda said. "I bet the Sacred Soil from the Su Nuraxi is in it."

"Stay with him. I think you're getting the information we need." The Headmaster was growing more confident that they could defeat the Sorcerer Corradhu despite the dangerous challenges ahead. They just needed time to plan their tactics.

Minda watched as the Sorcerer Corradhu walked toward the nagas and the granite pillar where his sapphire staff was embedded. When he was within reach of it, the nagas sat perfectly still and reverent as he approached. As he walked between them, he patted each of the nagas on the heads as if they were his pets. Both nuzzled against his hand.

"He's reaching for the sapphire staff," Minda began to describe what was happening. "He is going to withdraw it. Wait. He stopped. I think something has distracted him. He is grabbing the pouch with the soil. He just said, 'take me to the ritual clearing'. He is floating up over the treetops. The Sorcerer Corradhu has flown off quickly to the west." Minda lost contact with the Sorcerer Corradhu.

"He's going to the ritual clearing to await the return of the Eleven Sisters of the Coven," Professor O'Riley said.

"All but one," the Headmaster reminded the professor. "Minda, Remote View the ritual clearing. When he finds out Assunta failed to return, he may reveal something of use to us." The Headmaster and Professor O'Riley adjourned to a corner of the Headmaster's study saying they were giving Minda some room to focus on the ritual clearing.

The truth was, the Headmaster and Professor O'Riley wanted to discuss their next steps against the Sorcerer Corradhu out of earshot of Minda. Their main concern was not so much the Sapphire Staff and the Sacred Soil of Su Nuraxi, although they were important. They were more concerned about how to separate the Sorcerer Corradhu from the Sisters of the Coven. Professor O'Riley reminded the Headmaster that they didn't need to capture them all. As long as there were no more than two remaining, the curse could not be cast. But how? The witches of the Sisterhood were very, very accomplished witches. Capturing even one of them would be difficult and dangerous. Neither the Headmaster nor Professor O'Riley could think of anyone within the enchanter ranks who could be called upon. Professor O'Riley raised the possibility of Major Lisset as an option since she and her army were already on their way to Clonfert House. The Headmaster agreed.

It was easy for Minda to turn her Remote Viewing in the direction of the ritual clearing. With each passing hour her skill seemed to become stronger, clearer. She thought to herself, *if only I could Mind Mirror the Sorcerer Corradhu as I did with Michael during the capture of Uncle Rabbit in the basement of Saint Brendan's Cathedral. Now, that would put the Sorcerer Corradhu at a real disadvantage.* Try as she might, she just couldn't mirror the Sorcerer Corradhu's consciousness. Minda wondered if it was because he was a sorcerer or because he was so evil.

Chapter 14
The Eo Mugna Tree Affey Shares
Her Dream

Affey couldn't wait to go see the Green Maiden. Before she did, Affey went to her room to see for herself just how different she looked now that she was fully the eighth Green Maiden.

"My eyes! They are back to their usual color," Affey said as she examined them closely in the mirror. When her transition first began, the color of her eyes fluctuated from day to day. Because of this, she expected them to change color too. Maybe turn green, or gold, or hazel. They had not changed at all. They were still the same very dark brown — a trait she shared with her twin sister, Minda. Affey always liked the way the copper flecks in their glimmered when the light struck them just right. Now, those same copper flecks shimmered brighter than ever. She wondered if Minda would notice when they next met. Affey next turned her attention to her face.

She moved a bit closer to the mirror. Affey ran the tips of her fingers over her emerald cheeks. Affey's emerald skin was vibrant as if she had been buffed and polished. She wondered if her skin was so shiny that someone looking at her would see their reflection just like she was seeing hers in the mirror. The green of her skin was different than the Green Maiden's. The Green Maiden's skin became flatter and duller with each passing day. Affey asked the mirror, "Do all Green Maidens start out like I am now? Will I too start to fade as my time as Green Maiden draws to a close?" Affey stepped back and stood looking in the mirror asking herself the same questions over, and over again. It was tough for her to accept, yet she knew it was her destiny, just as it was the destiny of all Green Maidens. Affey was proud of how she looked. She was also humbled by how her essence and power naturally radiated from her.

Standing there looking at her spirit self in the mirror, it sunk in that with her transformation came heavy responsibility.

Affey leaned into the mirror again to closely examine the nape of her neck. She thought she saw something there. She leaned in even closer to the mirror to see what it was. As she traced a line from just underneath her chin, down over her throat she saw what it was. When she pressed her finger against her skin, even slightly, a brown hue blushed under her emerald skin like a shadow. It was barely visible, yet it was there. She pressed against her throat once, twice, three times. Each time the brown blush rose, but quickly faded when she stopped pressing her fingers against her skin. She next tried the same thing on her forearm, her wrist, her knee, her ankle, the top of her foot. Each time she pressed on her skin with her fingers, the brown blush appeared.

"I'm still in there," Affey said joyfully. "Underneath this emerald skin, Affey's chocolate skin is there. That means, I, Affey, twin sister of Minda Temne, am still here even though I am the eighth Green Maiden."

She stoked her dreadlocks. The braids were intertwined with gold, silver, and platinum. The threads made her hair look as if it was hung with stars. A sunbeam broke that through the branches above her room illuminated her hair. A rainbow of colors danced across the floor of her bedroom as if they had passed through a crystal prism.

"I am the eighth Green Maiden." The way she said the words proved that Affey now fully accepted her destiny. She squared her shoulders, stood up straight, examined herself in the mirror from head to toe and said, "This is how a Green Maiden carries herself."

"Yes, Affey. It is." The Green Maiden was standing in the entrance to Affey's room. She turned to face the Green Maiden whose beauty and power were fading. A single tear dropped from the corner of her eye.

"You are so beautiful, Affey. I was never as radiant as you are. I think it is because your powers will far exceed mine." The Green Maiden took Affey's hands in hers, "I cannot find the words to tell you how happy I am to see as the eighth Green Maiden. I know that in your hands, these hands, the Wind and the Woods will be well cared for. I can pass from this realm to the next in peace."

Affey embraced the Green Maiden. She held her tightly. Affey didn't want the Green Maiden to leave her. The Green Maiden also held tightly to their embrace. She was approaching her final days as the seventh Green Maiden. It was the Green Maiden who finally broke their embrace.

"We must get you ready, Affey. As you know, my time is drawing to its end."

Still holding on to the Green Maiden's hands Affey said, "I know, Green Maiden. Your skin loses some of its luster every day. You tire easily. I want to help you in any way I can." What Affey really wanted was for the Green Maiden to stay with her forever. "I love you, Green Maiden."

"I love you too, Affey." The Green Maiden changed the mood. "Let's do something special today to celebrate. Let's do something unexpected." The Green Maiden was livelier than Affey had seen her in some time.

"Like what," Affey asked enthusiastically.

The Green Maiden paused before she told Affey. She wanted her idea to take Affey by surprise.

"Let's go to Clonfert House and see your sister, Minda."

"Really?!" Affey was again on the verge of tears.

"Yes, really. Are you ready to show her how you have changed?"

"I am, Green Maiden. Minda should be the first to see me, don't you think?"

"Yes, Affey. Minda should be the first." The Green Maiden pushed aside thoughts of the Sorcerer Corradhu. She wanted Affey to take her time adjusting to her new spirit self. Taking Affey, the eighth Green Maiden, to Clonfert House was more important. They would address the issue of the Sorcerer Corradhu afterward.

"Botsam," the Green Maiden called out. Botsam appeared instantly as he always did. "Go to Clonfert House. Tell the Headmaster that I am coming today for a visit. I have something special to show him. Tell him I will only stay for a few hours. Inform him that I should arrive about an hour after you. Do not mention Affey at all."

"I'm on my way, Mistress. By the way, Affey, I mean Mistress. You look even more radiant than when you first woke up from your dream." Botsam departed for Clonfert House.

Before they left to visit Clonfert House, the Green Maiden took a Affey into the Green Maiden's Ritual Chamber. Affey had been in it before, but now she entered as its next occupant. Once inside they sat side-by-side. Together, speaking as one, they recited the invocations for a safe journey. When the recitation was over, the Green Maiden wanted to ask Affey about her initiation dream. The Green Maiden wanted to know if it was the same dream she and every other Green Maiden had for their initiations. The Green Maiden was also required to make a record of Affey's initiation for inclusion in the Annals of the Sisterhood.

"So, Affey, tell me about your dream. Were all the prior Green Maidens and Spirit Sisters there?"

"They were, Green Maiden."

"They are beautiful even after passing into the next realm, aren't they?" The Green Maiden said, looking for confirmation that she too would be restored to her former beauty once she departed this realm.

"No more beautiful than you are Green Maiden," Affey said with a smile.

"Thank you, Affey. That was very kind of you to say."

"The others had a rarer, more ethereal beauty," Affey said assuming the Green Maiden was going to ask about the Twenty-Two Celestial Sirens.

The Green Maiden was taken aback. "There were others there?"

"You seemed surprised, Green Maiden. Why?"

"I don't know of any initiation dream that involved by any beings other than the past Green Maidens and the Spirit Sisters. There is no mention in the Annals of the Sisterhood of any other beings. You must tell me everything. I have to make an accurate record of your dream." The Green Maiden sounded anxious about this. Affey thought that maybe she should not mention the Twenty-Two Celestial Sirens, but how was she to know their presence was unusual. Affey didn't know what, if anything more she should say.

"You are hesitating, Affey. Please, just tell me. Whoever these others were must have come because you are the first mortal to become Green Maiden."

"I am not hesitating, Green Maiden. I just don't know if I'm supposed to tell you, that's all."

"Why not?" asked the Green Maiden.

"Just a feeling."

"Affey, their presence in your dream is extraordinary. We must, for the sake of our history, record it in the annals." The Green Maiden would insist if she had to, but she hoped Affey would understand the historical importance of the presence of these others in her dream.

"They were the Twenty-Two Celestial Sirens."

"Really? Are you sure? The sirens have not descended from their realm in thousands of years. We must make a complete record of your dream."

"I'm sure, Green Maiden, that the prior Green Maidens and Spirit Sisters were as surprised, confused, and awestruck as you are. I don't think they knew what to do so, they kneeled out of respect, I guess. Then, for some reason I can't explain, they let the Twenty-Two Celestial Sirens take over. It was the sirens who performed the rituals, not the Green Maidens."

"Most extraordinary," was all the Green Maiden said as she wrote down all that Affey was reporting. Affey was able to recall everything about her dream. However, she left out one detail – the prophecy.

When Affey stopped speaking, the Green Maiden looked up from her writing and asked Affey. "Is that all? Are you sure that's everything.?"

Affey took several minutes to think about what she told the Green Maiden. She realized she forgot to mention her parents. "My parents were there at the end."

"That makes sense since you are human and have strong ties to your family. Anything else?" The Green Maiden had an inkling Affey left out something important.

"There is, Green Maiden. This time I really don't think I'm supposed to tell you."

"Let me ask you this, Affey. Do you think it is important to our history?"

Affey knew it was, so she told the Green Maiden, "there is one last thing. One of the Sirens, their leader, I think, told me I was the fulfillment of a prophecy."

"Affey, this prophecy may be the most important thing from you dream. Can you recall it?"

"I think I can." Affey recited the prophecy for the Green Maiden.

"There will be seven, in the old way.
The eighth begins anew.
She will rise up in the north
In a house of scholarship and secret.
Her emerald essence awakens swiftly,
Here birth nature cast off.
Beware the Dark Magician!
Triumph makes war with tragedy.

109

The emerald empress prevails
All worlds orbit as one."

The Green Maiden's eyes grew wider as Affey related the prophecy. When Affey finished, the Green Maiden spoke one, single word. She spoke it as if it the word were terror itself. "Corradhu!"

"Come Affey, we must go to Clonfert House without delay. I'm afraid our visit has taken on a new urgency."

Chapter 15
On the Way to Clonfert House
Affey Shares Her Doubts

Had the Green Maiden been going to Clonfert House by herself she would have used her power to materialize them there in an instant, but since Affey had not yet grown into that power, they had no choice but to travel by foot. Fortunately, it was a short journey of only a few hours. Along the way, the Green Maiden shared what she leaned from Master Foote. She had deliberately kept it from Affey's because Affey's transformation was more important. For her part, Affey was so caught up in her transformation, that she previously set aside what the Oracle of the Dar Lantern told her. But now, she used their journey as an opportunity to share the Oracle's prediction with the Green Maiden. They both realized that the prophecy concerning Affey was unfolding. It made them both a little tired. They took a short break to rest. When they were on their way again, Affey felt she that she had to share her doubts with the Green Maiden.

"Green Maiden, I have to tell you something."

"What is it, Affey? You seem a little upset."

Affey stopped walking and turned to face the Green Maiden. "I wouldn't say I'm upset exactly. It's more a combination of doubt, fear, and confusion."

The Green Maiden took Affey by the hand. "I share some of those same feelings. All of this, you becoming my successor, the arrival of the Sorcerer Corradhu, the prophecy. They frighten me. I think I'm suffering a bit of shock from all these events. Affey, I feel the approach of the end of my time as Green Maiden. I'm not myself."

"I know, Green Maiden. I can see it in your eyes. As I understand the prophesy, I think, in the end, it will fall upon me to drive out the Sorcerer Corradhu. I am not ready. I don't have the power. I'm just a teenager, even if I am a Green Maiden. Even as Green Maiden I am a novice. How am I supposed to repel this powerful sorcerer? The Oracle said lives would be lost. How can I live with that? It terrifies me. There is so much at stake."

"I know, Affey, I know. I too am overwhelmed by it all. Yet, you must find a way to put your feelings aside. You must trust the prophesy. Believe with all your heart that you will prevail."

"While I agree with you, Green Maiden, I lack your confidence."

"We will do this together, Affey," the Green Maiden said as they continued to walk toward Clonfert House. They didn't say much during the rest of the journey. Each was lost in their own thoughts.

The Green Maiden grew very tired. She tried her best to reassure Affey, but the truth was, the Greer Maiden didn't think she could be much help. She simply didn't have the strength. Her powers were fading more quickly than she anticipated. If she couldn't summon them, would Affey have not just the courage, but the power to face the Sorcerer Corradhu without her? As they got closer to Clonfert House, the Green Maiden couldn't decide how much of her thoughts she should share with Affey, or anyone at Clonfert House for that matter. For now, she decided to keep her thoughts to herself.

Affey's thoughts were no less troublesome. She could see that the Green Maiden was struggling. For the very first time it dawned on Affey that the Green Maiden may not be able to help her at all. If that were true, then Affey had to find some way to muster the resolve to go ahead without the Green Maiden. She noticed the Green Maiden was more tired. It was as if her thoughts were contributing to the Green Maiden's exhaustion.

Affey understood that she had no choice. It became very clear to her that this situation, thought fraught with dire consequences, was not that much different than what she had done in helping defeat Adena. However, there was one very crucial difference. This time she was the one who had to face the Sorcerer Corradhu, not the Headmaster. She asked herself, do I really have to do this alone? She recalled the words of the prophesy: *the emerald empress prevails*. It doesn't say I prevail alone, only that I prevail. Affey took this as a sign that she should enlist the help of others. Since she, Minda, Michael, and Kevin worked so well together before, she would bring them in. Perhaps others should be involved as well, but who? The Headmaster would have to be involved as would Professor O'Riley. What about the other professors or other students? What about Major Lisset and her female spirit warriors? Affey took a deep breath. She looked over to see how the Green Maiden was doing. She was struggling. Fortunately, Clonfert House was on the horizon. Affey slipped her arm into the Green Maiden's to help her along.

"Thank you Affey. I guess you can see I'm quite tired."

"You will be fine, Green Maiden. We are almost there."

***

"Headmaster! Headmaster!" The sentry from the main watch tower was knocking furiously at the Headmaster's study door.

"Enter," called out the Headmaster. He was used to these sudden announcements at his door. They very rarely were urgent. This one was different.

"Headmaster." The sentry had to pause to catch his breath. "The Green Maiden and a spirit girl are approaching on foot. I thought you would want to know immediately."

The sentry's announcement interrupted Minda's Remote Viewing of the Sorcerer Corradhu. "What did you say," she asked the sentry.

The Headmaster snapped at Minda and said sternly, "Stay with the Sorcerer!"

"Sorry, Headmaster, but if my sister is with the Green Maiden…"

The Headmaster raised his hand to silence her. "The sentry said there is a 'spirit girl' with the Green Maiden. This sentry knows Affey. He would have recognized her and said so. Please, Minda, get back to the Sorcerer Corradhu."

"Yes, Headmaster." Minda did as she was told, though she was not happy about it. She quickly reconnected with the Sorcerer Corradhu. He was pacing impatiently behind the altar in the ritual clearing ground awaiting the return of the Eleven Sisters of the Coven with their sacrificial spirits.

The Headmaster turned his attention back the sentry.

"Thank you. I appreciate your telling me. Now, go. Meet them and escort them here." The sentry left with the same urgency with which he had arrived.

Minda updated the Headmaster. "I have reconnected with the sorcerer, Headmaster. He is still waiting for the witches to return."

"Thank you, Minda. Just stay with him, no matter what."

"I'll do my best, Headmaster."

The Headmaster remained standing behind his desk waiting for the Green Maiden and her companion to arrive.

The Headmaster wondered why the Green Maiden had chosen to arrive on foot. Botsam didn't mention this or that she was bringing someone else with her. Who was this spirit girl that accompanied her? Did she have something to do with their visit. Most unusual indeed! Surely, she must have her reasons. He couldn't stop thinking about 'the spirit girl' the sentry mentioned. The Headmaster wondered if she was some new arrival in the Green Maiden's lair. The Green Maiden was attended by her guardians. The arrival of a 'spirit girl' was most unusual. Did it have something to do with the Sorcerer Corradhu? The Green Maiden would surely explain.

***

As they approached the main to Clonfert House, Affey recalled what the Oracle of the Dar Lantern told her. "Before this is all over with the Sorcerer Corradhu you will be severely tested. There will be times when you must insist others follow you. Some of them may refuse and you will have to decide what to do about them. Some of those decisions could be harmful. Some of those close to you may not survive this confrontation with the Sorcerer Corradhu." Affey felt that the Oracle had given her a check list of things she was to so. Some of them deeply disturbed her. She ran through the list in her head.

I must insist others follow me. Some will refuse. Who might they be? Surely not Minda, Michael, of Kevin. They were her closest friends. They followed her in the defeat of Adena. No doubt they would follow her again now. Would the Headmaster or Professor O'Riley object? What about the other professors? *They,* Affey thought, *would most likely be the obstacles.* She would just have to face that if or when the time came. *Next,* she thought, *I will have to make some difficult decisions. Like what,* she wondered? Again, she decided she would just have to wait and see how things unfolded. There will be losses, some will hurt me. Of all the predictions the Oracle made, this was the most difficult one for Affey. She absolutely refused to even think about losing Minda. She felt the same way about Michael and Kevin, but she would not feel their loss in the same way. Is it possible the Headmaster, Professor O'Riley or the other professors would suffer and die in this conflict? Affey thought that this was a more likely than the loss of Minda, Michael, or Kevin. At no point did Affey consider that the Green Maiden might be one of the losses. Lastly, in the end, she knew the sorcerer would be driven out. She said to herself, *I must put all me energy in driving him away. I will just have to put all my fears aside. There is no room for doubt or hesitation. I must remember the words of the prophecy: all worlds orbit as one.*

When she and the Green Maiden were no more than a few yards from the entrance to Clonfert House, the Green Maiden stumbled and fell. Affey picked her up and carried her the rest of the way.

The Green Maiden said, as they crossed through the entrance into Clonfert House, "you will know what to do, Affey. As a Green Maiden you are about to discover that this world, our universe, will always provide for you. Just listen for it. When it comes, follow it without hesitation. It is how we Green Maidens are aligned with the infinite universe."

At that moment Affey felt something pass between her and the Green Maiden. It was tangible, physical. It was also beyond words. The Green Maiden was right. In that split second of time, as she held the Green Maiden in her arms, she believed that she would know what to do and how to do it. An entire strategy unfolded before her. Tactics likewise were revealed. The Green Maiden was right. The universe did provide. It was time to confront the Sorcerer Corradhu. She was ready.

A sentry approached Affey and the Green Maiden. "I'm to bring you to the Headmaster."

"Please," Affey said. "Can you ask the infirmary to send someone to examine the Green Maiden. She is very, very tired."

"I will miss." The sentry led them to the Headmaster's study. Along the way the Green Maiden seemed to recover just a little.

"Please put me down, Affey. I don't want the Headmaster to see me like this. It might shake his confidence in us." Affey put her down as they reached the Headmaster's study.

The Green Maiden straightened her dress, smoothed her hair just before the Headmaster's door opened.

Chapter 16
Clonfert House, The Headmaster's Study Affey Takes Control

The sentry knocked on his door again. Minda quickly looked toward the door. It was still closed. The Headmaster shot her a stern look. She returned her attention to the Sorcerer Corradhu.

"Please come in."

Minda tried again to sneak a peek at the Green Maiden and the spirit girl, but the open door blocked her view. She didn't want the Headmaster to admonish her again, so she returned to Remote Viewing the sorcerer.

When the door opened the Headmaster first saw the Green Maiden. They exchanged a quick greeting. Then the Green Maiden stepped aside.

"Affey?" the Headmaster asked.

When Minda heard Affey's name she broke from her attention on the Sorcerer Corradhu and ran toward the person the Headmaster called Affey. When Minda saw her twin sister, she stopped abruptly a few feet away from her. This creature certainly resembled her sister, but the hair was wrong. Her green skin wasn't possible. This person, this 'spirit girl,' was shorter than Affey but the eyes – they were Affey's eyes, though sparkling in a way Minda had never seen before. There was an aura around her. She radiated power. She looked like a Green Maiden. *Not possible,* Minda thought. If this was her twin sister, then she had become something Minda couldn't fathom.

"Is it you, Affey? What has happened to you? Why are you like this?" Minda's tone was cautious, disbelieving. Affey was sad to hear her sister talk to her this way. She hoped that her first encounter as Green Maiden with Minda would be a joyful one. She was disappointed Minda didn't seem happy to see her no matter that she changed so dramatically. Was Minda one who would refuse to follow her?

Affey embraced her sister. She held her tightly and said, "I promise, Minda, I will tell you everything. There will be time for that later. Right now, must focus on the Sorcerer Corradhu. Everything else must wait."

Minda pulled slightly back from Affey's embrace. Her hands were still on Affey's shoulders. "You know about the Sorcerer Corradhu? How? Why?" Minda was alarmed that Affey was involved with the Sorcerer Corradhu. She wondered if Affey had any idea of the danger he presented.

Affey responded to her sister simply saying, "I do."

Minda wasn't sure what to say or do. Between Affey's radical change and her knowing about the Sorcerer Corradhu, Minda felt paralyzed.

Seeing the difficulty Minda was having, the Headmaster stepped between them. "Minda, please, return to your duty. We cannot afford to lose contact with the Sorcerer Corradhu." Minda looked to Affey for some direction.

"Do as the Headmaster asks, Minda. I will tell you everything. I promise." Minda reluctantly went back to her chair in the corner to Remote View the Sorcerer Corradhu. She found it hard to do it with Affey in the room. Yet, she knew she must and so she did. Affey took this a sign that she could count on her twin sister, just as she always had.

The Headmaster looked intently at Affey. To say he was astonished would not fully describe his reaction. Affey looked up at him with her sparkling gold flecked eyes in a way that so startled him that he took a step backward. Affey was no longer some naive student plucked from a minor academy. In fact, he wasn't sure much of Affey remained in this young Green Maiden. Like Minda, he wasn't sure what to say so he turned to the Green Maiden for help in understanding what had happened to Affey.

"She's obviously physically changed, Headmaster. She has changed in more ways than you can imagine. I know this must come as a shock to you since Affey is, or was, human after all. Yet, here she stands before you, a Green Maiden."

The Green Maiden's comment did nothing to ease his confusion. "This is most extraordinary. Unheard of, as far as I know."

What Affey did next forever altered her relationship with the Headmaster. It would not be the first relationship to change. She knew it was time to take control of the planning of the confrontation with the Sorcerer Corradhu. The Oracle of the Dar Lantern's words ran through her head: *there will come a time when you must insist others follow you – some will resist.* It was time to find out if the Headmaster was one of them.

Affey squared her shoulders, took a step closer to the Headmaster and addressed him not as his student, but as his peer.

"My dear Headmaster, I too was confused at first. Yet, in a matter of just a few days it all became quite clear to me. Shall we sit down?" Without waiting for the Headmaster to answer she sat on one side of his conference table with the Green Maiden. She gestured for the Headmaster to sit opposite them. He did as he was asked. Affey noted his compliance with her request. He would not be one of those to resist her.

She continued. "At first, we were coming to pay you, my sister, Michael, and Kevin a surprise visit to show all of you what has happened to me. However, as we are about to explain, our visit is no longer a social one. We are here to help expel the Sorcerer Corradhu."

The Green Maiden added, "I apologize for not telling you sooner, Headmaster. Everything happened so quickly. I too was troubled by Affey's change. I wasn't sure how to proceed. The Oracle of the Dar Lantern helped me understand."

The Headmaster was so intent on looking at Affey that he didn't pay any attention to what the Green Maiden said. If he did, then he would have asked more about what the Oracle said. Instead, he spoke only to Affey.

"Affey, you are so very, very different. I don't just mean your appearance. I see very little of Affey in you. I see only a blossoming Green Maiden. There is a power emanating from you that almost eclipses that of the Green Maiden. I do hope you or the Green Maiden can explain all this so that it makes some sense to me."

"We will," said the Green Maiden. "Please tell him about your initiation. It might help the Headmaster understand."

Mention of an initiation interfered with Minda's Remote Viewing of the Sorcerer Corradhu. She had been eavesdropping on Affey all along without any interference in her concentration, but this? This just was too much for Minda to ignore. Affey sensed it. Without even looking at her sister, she said, "don't worry, Minda, I will explain everything. I promise. Please, don't stray from Remote Viewing the sorcerer." Minda returned to observing the Sorcerer Corradhu. However, she had to fight the urge to sit by her sister so she could listen to everything she said. Minda knew that Remote Viewing the Sorcerer

Corradhu was crucial, but she was torn between the two. She did her best to stay with the Sorcerer Corradhu while at the same time continuing to eavesdrop on Affey.

Affey leaned forward on the conference table and held the Headmaster in her gaze. He was struck by the shimmering light he saw behind her eyes. It was more radiant and piercing than the current Green Maiden's. It was the second difference between Affey and the Green Maiden that he noticed. Briefly, he wondered what it meant. He shook off that thought. He folded his hands on the table and leaned forward as if to better hear what Affey had to say.

"Headmaster. While a full accounting of the last several days where I transformed from Affey into the Green Maiden is due you, it will have to wait for another day. We must join our efforts quickly if we are to expel the Sorcerer Corradhu from the Western Quarter, if not the whole world." Affey was intent on keeping everyone focused on the Sorcerer Corradhu and not herself.

The Headmaster sat back in his chair with a deep, resigned sigh. He was not going to get the explanation he wanted.

"We all know how important it is to drive away the Sorcerer Corradhu." He decided to try one more time to get an explanation from Affey or the Green Maiden. "What I don't understand is your role in all of this. What does his arrival in the Western Quarter have to do with you becoming a Green Maiden? I am very perplexed by this." The Headmaster was not often caught unaware of people, places, or events. Somehow, he didn't foresee what was unfolding before him. Neither the Green Maiden nor Affey had any idea of just how deeply disturbed the Headmaster was. Affey did sensed that something perturbed the Headmaster. She got up and went to sit beside him. He looked over at her with tired eyes. It was the same kind of weariness Affey saw in the Green Maiden's eyes. She spoke to him gently.

"Headmaster. Do not be concerned. The Sorcerer Corradhu will be defeated. I have no doubt about this. You must trust me. It will not be easy and there will be losses. Some of them will be difficult to accept, but they will not be in vain."

"How can you be so sure?" The Headmaster asked.

"There is a prophecy," the Green Maiden interjected.

This was too much for the Headmaster. He thought he was privy to every prophecy that involved the relationship between the human and spirit worlds.

He sat up straight in his chair. He was not pleased. He was slipping out of balance.

"What prophecy? I am not aware of any prophecy involving the Sorcerer Corradhu." Affey touched his shoulder to reassure him.

"Tell him, Affey," the Green Maiden said.

"Do you know of the Twenty-Two Celestial Sirens," Affey asked the Headmaster. He took it as a slight insult.

"Of course, I do. Are you now going to tell me they are involved in this as well? That I find very hard to believe. There has been no encounter with them for over a thousand years." The Headmaster was dismissive to the idea of the sirens suddenly appearing.

"Well, now there has been an encounter. It was with Affey," The Green Maiden said. The Headmaster was slacked jawed. He turned to Affey with a look on his face that demanded an explanation. Affey took it as such. She knew he needed more if he was going to follow her.

"During my initiation as Green Maiden the Twenty-Two Celestial Sirens arrived. In fact, they actually conducted my initiation ritual and not the former Green Maidens and Spirit Sisters as is the tradition."

The Headmaster sat back in his chair with his hand covering his mouth to stifle a gasp.

Affey continued. "At the end of the ritual one of sirens spoke the following prophecy to me. It is this prophecy that brings us to you today. This is what she said:

"There will be seven, in the old way.
The eighth begins anew.
She will rise up in the north
In a house of scholarship and secret.
Her emerald essence awakens swiftly.
Her birth nature cast off.
Beware the Dark Magician.
Triumph makes war with tragedy.
The emerald empress prevails.
All worlds orbit as one."

A heavy, leaden silence fell over the Headmaster's study. The Headmaster sat with his eyes closed. His mind whirling. He couldn't sort this all out. Affey and the Green Maiden waited for him to speak.

Over in the corner monitoring the Sorcerer Corradhu, Minda, took in everything Affey said. She became distraught when she heard the words, "triumph makes war with tragedy." Minda feared for her sister's life, but kept her fear to herself – for now.

The Headmaster opened his eyes. "This prophecy could not be any clearer, though it terrifies me."

"Why," Affey asked.

"Because my dearest Affey, or should I say, Green Maiden. This once more puts you at the center of dangerous circumstances. How do we know you are ready? There is so much to consider. Right now, I can only begin to imagine the implications of this prophecy. I believe they are more profound than perhaps you, or any of us, realize."

"That may be true," Affey said. "Our immediate responsibility is to confront the Sorcerer Corradhu and the Eleven Sisters of the Coven. We cannot become distracted by trying to predict the implications. They will reveal themselves soon enough." Affey stood up. The Headmaster and the Green Maiden stood as well. This was one more indication for Affey that the Headmaster would follow her.

"Affey, sorry, Green Maiden, there is something I must tell you." The Headmaster was going to tell them about Assunta.

"What is it," Affey asked.

"There are only ten sisters. One them, Assunta, has defected to us. She is horrified by the Sorcerer Corradhu's cruelty. We have questioned her, but she didn't have any useful information. She is staying with us for the time being."

Affey asked, "is she safe? Do you think she can be of any help at all?"

"I doubt it."

"Okay. You might want to set guards to protect her. Also, Headmaster, please summon Professor O'Riley, Michael, Kevin, and Gianni Giannotti."

The mentioned of Gianni Giannotti added one more unexpected item to the Headmaster's list of the unexpected.

"Giannotti? Why?" This made no sense to the Headmaster.

The Green Maiden too found his name unexpected. Affey had not mentioned him at all.

Affey explained. "Gianni has unusual sword skills, so I have been told. Those skills will be needed, though I'm not clear about just how yet." That was explanation enough for the Headmaster and the Green Maiden. "Now, please, summon them. We have no time to waste. Don't forget to set the guards for Assunta."

The Headmaster did as Affey instructed. Messengers were dispatched with orders to inform them that the Headmaster needed to see them immediately. No reason or explanation was to be given. No mention was to be made of Affey or the Green Maiden. Soon, they would all arrive. They were about to meet Affey, the new Green Maiden.

Minda spoke up from. Her corner of the study. "The Sorcerer Corradhu's mood has changed. He stopped pacing. He's standing at the ritual altar. I think something is about to happen."

Chapter 17

Clonfert House Deep into the Eastern Forest Kevin Meets the Ancient Man

Kevin worked tirelessly in the clearing in the Eastern Forest where the Headmaster took him to practice. He devised a variety of ways to bend and weave the trees and shrubs into an inescapable dome and impenetrable walls that would ensnare the Sorcerer Corradhu and anything or anyone under it. Try as he might, each of Kevin's attempts was flawed in some way. Each time, just when he thought he succeeded, he watched as a sparrow, raven, squirrel, or other creature, found some route through into the freedom of the open air. Over and over, and over again. he tried. One time, in a fit of frustration, he let loose so much energy that he snapped several ancient oaks and maples in half, scaring the birds from the branches. The underbrush was in disarray. This so upset him that he seriously considered abandoning all further attempts. He would just return to the Clonfert House, admit his failure, and suffer the consequences. As he sat on the ground trying to summon up the courage to return to the Headmaster and confess his failure, a nymph suddenly perched on a nearby rock.

Kevin had few encounters with the spirit world. He wasn't sure what to make of the nymph's arrival. Kevin couldn't tell if the nymph was male or female. He couldn't even begin to guess its age. The nymph was shabbily dressed in drab autumnal colors; a mottled combination of faded brown, amber, orange, and red. Its face was dirty. Its hair the color of wet straw. *Surely,* Kevin thought, *this nymph is no noble spirit.*

"Master Kevin? You are Master Kevin of Clonfert House are you not?"

"Maybe. Who are you?" Kevin was suspicious. How did he know his name How did he know he was in the Eastern Forest? Did he know what Kevin was doing? Was this some test from the Headmaster or some spirit mischief?

The nymph flew up to a branch just above Kevin's head. "Who I am doesn't matter, Kevin. You'd soon forget it anyway." The nymph teased Kevin. "Having a few problems are you, Kevin?"

Kevin stood up to get away from the nymph. He didn't have time for this even if it was a test. He particularly didn't like the way the nymph said his name as a kind of punctuation mark at the end of its sentences.

"I'll figure it out. Leave me alone. Go away." The nymph followed Kevin as he walked away. It kept flittering around and talking over Kevin's shoulder.

"You know, I can help you, Kevin."

"Really? I don't think I need your help." Kevin wanted the nymph to leave him alone. "I just need to practice more."

"So, does that mean you're not going back to Clonfert House, Kevin? Have you decided not to tell the Headmaster you're a failure, Kevin?" This stopped Kevin in his tracks. He tried to swat at the nymph, but it was too quick for him. It just flitted away a few feet beyond Kevin's reach.

"What?! How do you know that?" Kevin demanded. The nymph ignored his demand.

"I know a lot of things, Kevin. But right now, Kevin, you should be asking me how I know I can help you."

Kevin sat down on the ground confused and frustrated. The nymph landed on the ground in front of him. He was a rather tiny spirit. Kevin had to lean over his knees to see it.

The nymph stood with its hands on its hips. "Well, Kevin, what will it be? Help or failure?"

Kevin looked at the little nymph for a long time without answering. He didn't want to return to Clonfert House a failure. On the other hand, he had no clue who this nymph was or if he should trust it. He wasn't sure what to do.

"I see you are having a difficult time deciding, Kevin."

"Of course, I am, you, you, whoever of whatever you are. I fail at this, and I'm finished at Clonfert House."

The nymph hovered very close to Kevin's face. He leaned in so close, he almost touched Kevin's nose. He scolded Kevin.

"You only think about yourself, Kevin. If you fail, the Sorcerer Corradhu will prevail. The Western Quarter lost. Many will die. It will be just the first of the many horrors he will inflict on the spirit realms. The human realm will be next. Snap out of it, Kevin!" The nymph slapped Kevin hard on the nose. It hurt even though the nymph's hands were so tiny. Kevin tried again to flick the nymph away. He missed.

"Failed again, Kevin." The nymph flew away laughing just beyond Kevin's reach. *Maybe I should just give up, or maybe give in,* Kevin thought. The nymph stopped mid-flight and turned around to look at Kevin.

Kevin resented this annoying little creature who seem to be able to read his mind. He hated the way he kept repeating Kevin's name. "Say my name one more time and I swear I will…"

"Do what? You can't harm me." The nymph flew right up to Kevin's face again and said, "Kevin!" It laughed entirely too loud for a small creature.

"Alright, alright. You win. How can you help me?" Kevin decided to give in to the nymph. Giving it a chance to help was better than returning to Clonfert House a failure. At least he could say he tried, just in case this was a test from the Headmaster. What did he have to lose?

Kevin's change of heart affected a sudden change in the nymph. It changed colors. Its clothes turned vibrant green, gold, yellow, amber, crimson, rust, all the summer colors of the Eastern Forest. Its skin was wiped clean. The nymph's hair changed from a wet hay to a luxurious gold. Its attitude toward Kevin also was different.

"It's much easier than you think, Kevin. And, just so you know, the reason I keep saying your name is to remind you to pay attention. Now, follow me." The nymph led Kevin toward the center of the clearing in the Eastern Forest.

Once they were there, the nymph floated motionless in mid-air. Kevin had never seen anything so alive and yet so still. Kevin kept shifting on his feet. His knees were trembling. The nymph opened one eye to give Kevin a sideways glance. "Stand as still as you can, Kevin. He won't come unless you do."

"What? Who?" Kevin didn't know if he should stay or run away.

"The one who sent me to you."

Kevin was too scared and confused to run. He did his best to mimic the nymph's stillness, but his knees wouldn't stop shaking. Was whoever coming good or evil? The nymph said he was coming help to him.

"Stand still, Kevin!" the nymph ordered.

Kevin took several deep breaths. They helped calm his shaking knees. He was able to become almost as still as the nymph. A soft, fragrant breeze stirred the air around them. At first, Kevin wasn't sure if he heard the voice or if he imagined it. Then he felt a hand touch his knee.

"Open your eyes, Kevin. You too nymph."

Kevin looked down to see standing before him, an ancient man. He was quite small, but not as nearly small as the nymph. He was just over three feet tall. Kevin wasn't sure if he was even a spirit. The Ancient Man was dressed in a tattered brown over coat that was much too big for him. His grey hair and beard reached the ground. He leaned his leathered hands on a crooked walking stick. He wore no shoes. Though he was very, very old, he had more vitality than most people Kevin had ever met, even those his own age.

"I'm glad you listened to my nymph. He can sometimes be very persuasive. I don't usually concern myself in matters such as the one you, Clonfert House, and the spirits are currently engaged with. I find them tiresome. Besides, they eventually come to an end. This time things are different, Kevin. This Sorcerer Corradhu and the Eleven Sisters of the Coven must be expelled and driven back to where they came from. If they are not, then all spirit realms will be destroyed. There will be no recovering from this. He won't stop with the spirits. He will set his sights on the human realm after that."

"So, that is why you are here to help me?"

"It is, Kevin, you must be the first to succeed in your task. Everything else depends on it."

Kevin had not realized the gravity of his assignment. *Now,* he thought to himself, *I absolutely must figure out how to weave the dome and the walls. There is no room for failure. There can't be any excuses.*

The Ancient Man continued. "I have been watching you. Success is almost within your reach. You are missing only one element. Without this element you will never succeed. Failure will be your only result. The Sorcerer Corradhu and The Eleven Sisters of the Coven will prevail. Find this element, and your power over this forest, indeed all forests, will be formidable."

"Are you going to give it to me or tell me how to find it," Kevin asked.

The Ancient Man took a step closer to Kevin. He looked up at him with searching eyes. Kevin tried to step back, but the ancient man grabbed his wrist stopping him. His grip was surprisingly strong. Kevin yielded to it. The Ancient Man said, "ah, you see. There is your problem. You think this missing element is a thing, some totem, to be given to you or found hidden on some forest path. The truth is, you already have it. You just don't recognize it. You are putting up an obstacle to its discovery."

Kevin became even more confused. How could he possibly already have the one missing thing he needed to bend, twist, and weave the forest into an inescapable, impenetrable dome and walls?

The Ancient Man let go of Kevin's wrist and leaned on his crooked walking stick. "Answer me this, Kevin. When you first tried to weave the dome, what was the very first thing you thought? The very first thing."

The answer came to Kevin immediately. He said without any hesitation. "That's easy. From the start I didn't think I could do this. The more I tried, the more I doubted myself."

"Repeat what you just said," the nymph chimed in.

"I doubted myself."

The Ancient Man smiled but didn't say a word. He needed Kevin to listen to himself. To hear, really hear what Kevin just admitted to himself. As he watched Kevin come to understand, the Ancient Man saw the exact moment of Kevin's realization. It was as if Kevin grew taller, straighter, stronger.

"Doubt." Kevin said quietly. "I doubted myself. That is the obstacle."

The Ancient Man was pleased. "Doubt you certainly had, Kevin. You are right in saying that is the obstacle that keeps getting in your way." Then he asked Kevin the question that would lead Kevin to the missing element crucial to his success.

"What do find when you erase the doubt?" The Ancient Man watched Kevin closely once again for the moment of Kevin's realization.

Kevin smiled. Shook his head in disbelief. How did miss it? It was right within his reach all along. Kevin took a deep breath.

"Conviction," he said. "The missing element is conviction."

The Ancient tan tapped Kevin on the knee. "Ah, there it is. Conviction. You must be convinced you will succeed." The Ancient Man's work was done. He waved his leathery hands in the air as if casting a spell. Kevin's eyes closed. When Kevin opened his eyes, the Ancient Man and the nymph were gone.

"I can do this," he announced to the Eastern Forest.

Kevin raised his arms and began to bend the forest to his will. He was a conductor of a forest symphony of bending and weaving. Each branch struck the perfect note to bind and lift the dome above the clearing. Shrubs along the periphery moved and swayed in harmony to seal every exit from the clearing.

A final crescendo of light and energy burst from Kevin. He ended his construction with a single, magnificent bolt of lightning. No living thing could enter or leave unless he allowed it.

"I am ready for you, Sorcerer Corradhu and your witches!" he shouted. He released the trees, branches, and shrubs from the dome. They returned to their natural state He thanked them profoundly. Just then the messenger from the Headmaster arrived summoning him back to Clonfert House.

Chapter 18
The Sorcerer Corradhu's Ritual Clearing Ground The Sisters of the Coven Return

The Sorcerer Corradhu stopped pacing behind the ritual altar. The air in the ritual clearing crackled with an ominous energy. The Sisters of the Coven were about to return. He was anxious to see what sacrificial spirits they would bring him.

The first two sisters arrived.

"Show me, sisters," the Sorcerer Corradhu commanded. He stood on the edge of the ritual platform, the altar behind him.

The first sister approached him with her head bowed, her arm extended holding the cage up so the Sorcerer Corradhu could examine her offering. Inside her cage, was a kelpie sloshing inside a glass orb. When the Sorcerer Corradhu approached, the helpless kelpie swam frantically in circles.

The Sorcerer Corradhu was not pleased. "You bring me a kelpie? What were you thinking? How can I conduct the ritual with a water spirit? It will perish as soon as it is removed from this watery orb. You have failed me. You are a disappointment. I should banish you from the coven."

The sister started back away from the Sorcerer Corradhu with the caged kelpie.

"Leave it here," he said pointing to the altar. The sister did as she was told then retreated to the farthest edge of the clearing. She wanted to stay as far away from the sorcerer as she could. He turned to the second sister.

"I hope you have something of use to offer me."

She crept up to him exactly as the first sister had. Her arm outstretched, holding up her caged spirit. This spirit, a male elf, stood holding the bars of his cage defiantly. Before the Sorcerer Corradhu spoke the elf said, "so, you're the famous sorcerer. You don't look that powerful to me."

The Sorcerer Corradhu held the cage up slightly above his head. "You think so, do you?" With that, the sorcerer shook the caged violently sending the elf careening against the sides of the cage. He placed the cage on the altar. The elf fell to the floor of the cage dizzy. He wanted to vomit but wasn't about to give the Sorcerer Corradhu the satisfaction.

"Sister, I like this elf you have brought me. He's feisty. He will put up a fight. This pleases me."

The second sister stepped backward and knelt on the ground just off the edge of the ritual platform to the left of where the Sorcerer Corradhu stood. She was pleased with herself.

One by one the remaining sisters returned. Except for Assunta, whose absence was not immediately noticed.

Three of the sisters brought fairies. They cried and whimpered from the corners of their cages. The Sorcerer Corradhu was pleased with what these sisters brought him.

Another sister arrived dragging a small rope bound ogre who was too big for a cage. He hissed and spit at the sister. He stopped long enough when he was presented to the Sorcerer Corradhu to spit directly into the sorcerer's eyes. It was the last thing the ogre did. The Sorcerer Corradhu grabbed the ogre, snapped its neck, and tossed its lifeless body into the forest. The sisters recoiled. They were horrified by the sorcerer's violence.

The next sister, who arrived after the incident with the ogre, presented the sorcerer with one of the tiniest gnomes he had ever seen. The sister had to add extra webbing to the cage to keep it from escaping between the bars.

"Well," said the Sorcerer Corradhu holding up the cage to examine the gnome, "aren't you a treasure. You might just be my first sacrifice."

The tiny gnome, a female, stepped timidly up the edge of her cage. "I do hope not, your majesty." She didn't know what else to call him. She was trying to ingratiate herself with him. She thought addressing him as 'your majesty' might work. "I have special talents that you might find useful." She smiled up at him.

"Really? You think you have something I don't?" He laughed loudly then flung her cage against the base of the altar knocking the gnome unconscious.

It would take over an hour for her to recover. Once again, the sisters were taken back by the sorcerer's sudden violence.

Three sisters arrived together carrying a single cage covered in a silver cloth. "Father Corradhu, we have captured something quite special."

"Yes, sisters. Show me."

They approached him together. Instead of handing him the cage, they walked around to the other side of the altar. The carefully set it down directly in the center on top of the altar. They knelt to wait for the sorcerer to uncover the cage. He stepped to the other side of the altar so that when he uncovered the cage all the sisters could see what it contained. Before he lifted the silver cloth entirely, he raised it just enough to peek inside to see what they brought him. He raised his head slightly, smiled at the sisters sinisterly, and swept off the silver cloth in a single, swift motion. The other sisters gasped. Inside the cage was a leprechaun. They had been taught to have no contact with leprechauns. They were dangerous to witches. Just being in their presence could mean the onset of unbearable pain or even death. The sisters started to scuttle away from the altar platform.

"Stay right where you are," the Sorcerer Corradhu commanded. "I'm not afraid of some leprechaun. They hold no sway over me." He leaned down close to the leprechaun in the cage and said, "do you?"

The leprechaun, a female with flaming red hair and piercing blue eyes, remained seated in the middle of her cage. The whole time the Sorcerer Corradhu spoke she stared at him, humming a happy tune.

"You have nothing to say to me, miss?" His face was very close to the cage.

The leprechaun stood up, brushed off her dress, stepped right up to the bars of her cage and spat at him.

"Oh, no," one of the sisters said loud enough for them all to hear. They all thought this poor leprechaun would be yanked from her cage, have her neck snapped, and be tossed aside lifelessly just like the ogre. Their eyes were fixed on the Sorcerer Corradhu. He stepped back from the cage, wiped the spittle from his face, and let out a hearty laugh. It was the only way he could control his rage. Even though he didn't think the leprechaun had any power of him, he wasn't going to take any chances. She would be spared the ogre's fate. He held up the leprechaun's cage and announced.

"She will be the first one sacrificed in the morning." This came as a surprise to the sisters. They thought they each had to offer their individual spirits as the next sacrifice. He told that they each had to guarantee their spirit would not escape. Either he forgot, or he was fixated on the leprechaun. It didn't matter to the sisters which one it was. They were spared. For now.

Another sister arrived with two fairies in her cage. When she approached the Sorcerer Corradhu to present them to him, he wasn't interested. He pointed to a place on the altar where she should place her captives. He was too busy counting heads. None of the sisters had paid any attention to who had or had not arrived. Assunta was missing. As they watched him counting, they grew silent and anxious. One of them whispered, "where's Assunta? I don't see her."

"You don't see her because she is not here." The Sorcerer Corradhu stopped counting. His jaw was tightly set. He was so angry that the air around him sparked ferociously, something the sisters had never witnessed before. This was a terrible omen.

"We shall wait another ten minutes. If she is not here by then we will go and hunt her down." The sisters were appalled when he said, "hunt her down."

"I'm sure she will come," one of the sisters said. "She must have something special for you. It is just taking her a little more time to make her way back. She wouldn't abandon you."

Again, the Sorcerer Corradhu laughed aloud. "You would all abandon me if you thought you could get away with it."

They carried out, "no, father. Never." The Sorcerer had never spoken to the coven like that.

The Sorcerer Corradhu stood at the altar. He kept his eyes fixed on the sky above the trees looking for Assunta to arrive. Small, intense bursts of light circled around him. The smell of burning coal wafted through the air. The sisters huddled together fearful of what would come next. The leprechaun was unphased by it all. She sat quietly in the cage humming her pleasant tune.

The minutes ticked by. The Sorcerer Corradhu didn't budge and neither did the sisters. When the ten minutes had passed, the Sorcerer Corradhu had had enough of waiting.

"Sisters Philomena, Julietta, and Anna, you three are to scour the southern quarter looking for her. Theresa, Magdalena, Patrice, and Monica, you four are to search the eastern quarter. The other three of you are to head north. I want you to go directly to that cursed Clonfert House to see if there are any signs of her there. If any of you find her you are to do nothing. I mean nothing. One of you stay near her. The others are to return here to inform me of your findings. I will deal with her myself. Now, go and be quick about it."

The sisters didn't have to be told twice. They were so afraid for their lives that they all flew off to their assigned areas. The three dispatched to Clonfert House didn't want to go. The thought of human contact disgusted them. They had no choice but to follow the sorcerer's command.

The Sorcerer Corradhu transferred all he caged spirits to a large, metal box that sat under the altar. They wept as he did so. Except for the leprechaun. She kept humming her song. Once he was finished transferring them to the box, he closed the lid and locked it securely. The poor spirits were alone in the dark of the metal box. He headed back to his private encampment to retrieve his sapphire staff. He needed it if he was to summon all his powers in the ritual clearing.

The Sorcerer Corradhu was so pre-occupied with locking up the spirits that he didn't notice that he dropped the pouch with the Sacred Soil from the Su Nuraxi that hung on his belt into the box. It landed next to the leprechaun's cage. Once she was sure he was gone, she reached through the bars of her cage to grab it. It was too dark for any of the other spirits to notice. She quietly loosened the leather cord that cinched at the top of the pouch. She carefully peered inside. "Dirt," she whispered. She sniffed it. Nothing special about the smell. *Still,* she thought, *there is something about this soil that is important, otherwise why would he carry it?* She slipped it behind her to keep it hidden as best she could. It would have some use to her later. She hoped.

All the spirits wept and cried out, but not the leprechaun. She continued to sit in the darkness with the sorcerer's pouch. She continued humming her pleasant song. One of the elves in a nearby cage couldn't believe she was not as terrified as the rest of them.

"How can you keep humming a joyful song? Don't you realize that we are all going to be tortured and probably killed?"

The leprechaun stopped humming. She spoke to all the spirits trapped in the dark chest. "You must have faith that we will be rescued. I do. I've heard a rumor that the last spirit to be tortured was rescued. I believe we will as well. It would be best for you to quiet down. You will need all your strength when the rescuers come. You must be ready to flee with them."

"You're a leprechaun. You have a special king of magic. Can't you set us all free," came a voice from one of the cages.

"If I could, I already would have. My magic doesn't seem to work here. Still, I have to believe that we will be rescued." She went back to her humming. The other spirits quieted down, although some continued to whimper in the corners of their cages. She pulled the pouch of soil around to place it in her lap. "You, precious bag of dirt, you are going to help us escape, aren't you?"

Chapter 19
Clonfert House, The Headmaster's Study Affey's Plan

One by one they began to arrive at the Headmaster's study. Professor O'Riley was the first to arrive. The Headmaster met him at the door.

"Professor, I have something extraordinary to show, please come in." The Headmaster stepped aside. Affey was standing behind him. "May I introduce you to…"

"I know who she is," Professor O'Riley said even though the look on his face was one of complete surprise. "How could I not recognize those shining eyes." He and Affey smiled at each other. Professor O'Riley made a small bow to acknowledge her new status. "What a splendid Green Maiden you will be."

The Headmaster didn't understand the professor's reaction. "Aren't you shocked by what has happened to her?"

"Not all, Headmaster. From the first time she set foot in my office I expected something extraordinary from Affey. Maybe not this. She has certainly exceeded my expectations." He asked Affey, "how does being a Green Maiden suit you, Affey?"

"It's only been a few days, Professor. I'm still adjusting. I think I have a long way to go before I can answer you. With everything that's happening I haven't had time to think about it."

Professor O'Riley chuckled. The Headmaster only became more confused. Professor O'Riley asked the Headmaster, "why have you called me away from my work?"

"It's best if you ask Affey." The Headmaster sat down behind his desk to try to sort out what was happening. It was all very confusing.

"Let's sit down," Affey said as she led Professor O'Riley to the conference table.

Minda kept Remote Viewing the Sorcerer Corradhu, but she also eavesdropped on everything Affey said.

Once they were seated Affey asked Professor O'Riley. "Are you aware of the presence of the Sorcerer Corradhu in the Western Quarter?"

"I am and I know of his curse. What does that have to do with what has happened to you? Why are you here? Why did you bring up the sorcerer?" The professor looked over to the Headmaster for an explanation. The Headmaster shrugged his shoulders. This was not the reaction the Professor expected. It was disconcerting.

The Green Maiden, who was sitting next to Affey trying to gather what little strength she had left. She spoke to the professor.

"Professor, we do not have the luxury of time to explain. Let me just tell you that Affey's becoming a Green Maiden is the fulfillment of a prophecy. One that I had no knowledge of. When there is time and opportunity, we can share more about it. For now…" Her comments, though brief, exhausted the Green Maiden. She collapsed against the back of her chair. She could say no more. Affey tried to help her.

"Please, Green Maiden, rest. I can handle things. I will need you soon enough. Conserve your strength." Affey helped Professor O'Riley move the Green Maiden to a large over-stuffed chair in a corner of the study. She wrapped a blanket around the Green Maiden. The Green Maiden touched Affey's emerald cheek. "I will, Affey. I will." She closed her eyes and drifted off to a restless sleep.

Just as Affey was about to go back to her seat at the table Kevin arrived. He saw Affey, but didn't recognize her. He extended his hand to introduce himself.

"Hello, my name is Kevin, and…" He stopped mid-sentence. His eyes grew wide. He looked back and forth between the Headmaster and Professor O'Riley several times. They didn't say anything. Kevin turned back to Affey. He looked her over from head to toe in disbelief.

"No! This can't be." Affey just smiled at him. "Affey? Affey? Is it really you?"

"Kevin, the expression on your face is priceless." Affey laughed aloud. "I don't think I'll ever forget it." She stood on tip toe and threw her arms around Kevin. He wasn't sure what to do. "Give me a hug, Kevin." He held her tightly. As they stood together Affey whispered in Kevin's ear.

"Yes, my dear, dear Kevin, it is me, Affey. I have missed you."

He whispered back. "I've missed you too. Why are you disguised as a Green Maiden? By the way, it's a great disguise. It fooled me. How did you make yourself look smaller?"

Affey pulled back from their embrace. "It's not a disguise, Kevin. This is who I am now."

"I don't get it."

"You will, Kevin. When we have time, I'll tell you all about it."

"Can't you just tell me now?" He was pleading for an answer.

"In good time, Kevin. Let's sit down. There are important things we must talk about." He followed her to the table.

Before he sat down, he asked her, "Does this have anything to do with the Sorcerer Corradhu?"

"Yes, it does." Affey pointed to the seat next to her. "Sit next to me." He did.

"Everything okay, Minda?" Affey asked her sister. She didn't want Minda to feel left out. She also didn't want Minda to lose her focus on the Sorcerer Corradhu.

"He's still pacing. That's about it."

The Green Maiden moaned in her chair. Affey sprung up to go to her. The Headmaster, Kevin, and Professor O'Riley quickly followed.

"What's the matter, Green Maiden," Affey said as she knelt on the floor at the Green Maiden's feet.

"I'm fine. Just needed to take a deep breath. It came out as a moan. Sorry I disturbed you. I'm fine. Really." The Green Maiden pulled the cover up under chin and closed her eyes. Affey and the others returned to the table. Affey kept an eye her.

"I don't like how she looks," the Headmaster said.

"I think we should get her to the medical wing," Professor O'Riley offered. Both he and the Headmaster deferred to Affey for what should be done. Affey took it as sign they would not resist her.

"Call the infirmarian. Let's move her. She'll be more comfortable than in that chair. I'll tell her." Affey went and told the Green Maiden that she was going to the medical wing. The Green Maiden didn't object. The infirmarian arrived. He picked up the Green Maiden in his arms and carried her back to the medical wing of Clonfert House. There, she curled up in bed and slept soundly for many, many hours.

Gianni Giannotti arrived next. In his typical fashion, he sauntered through the Headmaster's door with his lavender scarf flapping over his shoulder. Affey went to greet him. His reaction to Affey was no different than the others, although it was more direct.

"Oh, child! How green you are. You've shrunk." He walked around her touching her shoulder, her hair. He came around to face her, threw his arms wide and said, "give us a hug."

Affey embraced him willingly. She was delighted to see him. While they hugged, Gianni glanced at those seated at the conference table. He was intrigued by their presence. He stepped back from their hug chagrined they had witnessed his greeting of Affey. He pulled her back into the hug and said quietly, "What's this all about? Why am I here?"

Affey told him in words she knew would get his attention. Gianni loved statements that were literary or fanciful, "Something is a foot. You must help."

That got him. He broke their hug. "Well, then. I am at your service." He bowed deeply, lifted his eyes to her and said, "Green Maiden." He was the first to address her in that way.

"Thank you, Gianni. Let's have seat with the others." Before they could sit down Michael arrived.

His reaction to Affey was the most unusual of all. He walked through the door and went directly to an open seat. Before he sat down, he turned to Affey.

"Hello, Affey. I see you are now a Green Maiden. Congratulations." He sat down. Professor O'Riley was flummoxed by Michael's apparent knowledge of Affey's transformation. The Headmaster was speechless.

Professor O'Riley asked Michael. "How, Michael? How did you know? None of us knew."

Michael was, by reputation, shier than his friends. He never boasted even if he had a good reason. This time, he didn't hesitate.

"I've had another visit from Master Bromley."

Professor O'Riley nearly fainted in his chair. He had only met Master Bromley twice, and one of those times was with Michael. Too many unexpected things were happening. The professor didn't like it one bit. Neither did the Headmaster, but he was too perplexed to say it.

Affey asked, "who is Master Bromley?"

Professor O'Riley shook off his astonishment at Michael's revelation and said, "he is the supervisor of the Secret Library. A fairy. I have only met him twice in my entire life. This is highly unusual."

Michael didn't respond.

"What did he tell you," Affey inquired. She did not have time for an explanation as to who or what Master Bromley was.

"He told me several things."

"Like what," Gianni said a bit annoyed that Michael was now the focus of everyone's attention. He didn't care who this Master Bromley was.

"First, he told me there was a prophecy about Affey becoming a Green Maiden. He said it was from a long, long time ago. It said it was mentioned in volume 962. The one that has gone missing from the Secret Library."

For the first time since she arrived at Clonfert House Affey was concerned by Michael's words. Missing volumes. Secret Library. A mysterious Master Bromley. It made her very uncomfortable.

"What is volume 962? Why is it missing? Is that important?"

They all heard the concern in her voice. Even Minda, locked on to the Sorcerer Corradhu, took notice.

Professor O'Riley tried to explain without saying more than necessary.

"It's a volume that somehow relates to our current state of affairs. Oddly, it is the only volume missing from the Secret Library. Master Bromley claims to know its contents." The professor emphasized the word 'claims'.

Michael disagreed. "I think it's more than that, professor. He knows everything that's in it. I believe him when he says so. In fact, he told me to remind you, and to inform Affey in particular, of something he told me, you professor, and you too Headmaster when he visited is in the Secret Library."

"I don't recall him saying anything to us that was…" The Headmaster lost his train of thought.

Michael ignored the Headmaster and spoke directly to Affey.

"Master Bromley told me to tell you, Affey, that the nagas guarding the Sorcerer Corradhu's sapphire staff can only be slain by cutting off their tails. He said that it is also mentioned in the Sacred Fairy Scrolls. Scroll 54, to be exact. I have no idea why he told me that, but he insisted that I tell you."

"Thank you, Michael. I think I know why, although having it come from a mysterious man whom I do not know is quite odd. I will tell you all in just a minute." She wanted to check-in with Minda.

"Anything, Minda?"

"Just the same. He's pacing and waiting."

"Okay," Gianni said in a huff. "I need to know more."

"Giannotti!" Professor O 'Riley chided Gianni.

"It's okay, Professor. Now that we are all here, I can explain." Affey sat still for several long minutes. The others were riveted on her. Kevin's knees bounced. Gianni fidgeted with his lavender scarf, Professor O'Riley scratched his head. The Headmaster stroked his beard. Affey opened her eyes. They all stopped what they were doing to listen.

"We must move against the Sorcerer Corradhu without delay. Each of us has a role to play in his defeat. When the Green Maiden and I were on our way here, there came a moment when an entire strategy and set of tactics just came to me. I have no idea how. They just did. I had no idea if they were what we needed or not. Now that Michael has delivered the message from Master Bromley, I have the confirmation I needed that what was shown to me is the right way to go."

"You mean about the nagas," Gianni asked.

"Yes, Gianni, it does. It also confirms the other things as well. Dealing with the nagas is where you and Kevin come in." She looked to Kevin to see if his knees were still shaking. Of course, they were.

"Kevin and I? He's just a teenager." Gianni objected to being tied to Kevin for something that was going to be dangerous. He didn't think Kevin was up to it.

Affey looked at Gianni with a steely expression. "Without him, you will fail."

Her words had such a profound effect on Gianni that he apologized to her and Kevin. To reassure Gianni and boost his ego she said, "I have asked you here because we need you and only you to assault the nagas, though you cannot go alone. I have been told that you are an exceptional swordsman. Am I right?"

"Some say so," he said with a false humility.

"Don't be so modest, Gianni," Affey said. "You heard what Michael said. The nagas tails must be severed. That is for you to accomplish with your unexcelled sword skills. For his part, Kevin has a method to entrap them right where they are. Am I right, Kevin? Together, you two must not just slay the nagas, but you must seize the Sorcerer Corradhu's sapphire staff which the nagas guard. You must bring it back here. It sits between them embedded in a granite block. They will fight to the death to protect it."

"How very Arthurian. A Sword-in-the-Stone," Gianni said. He was about to say something else when Minda said loud enough for all of them to hear, "Oh, no!"

"What is it," Affey asked her sister.

"I haven't said much because up until now nothing much has happened. The Sisters of the Coven have started to come back with their captive spirits. They are presenting them to the Sorcerer Corradhu. He seems pleased with most of what they have presented him, although he was very angry at an ogre one of the sisters offered. He viciously killed it and tossed it into the forest." Michael drew in a deep breath. The Headmaster stood up in disbelief. Kevin trembled. Professor O'Riley fell back into his chair. Gianni Giannotti covered his eyes and leaned forward on the table.

"Just now," Minda went on, "he realized Assunta is missing. He has sent the witches out to find her. Some to the east, some to the south, and three are headed here."

Affey thought to herself, *it's time. They either follow me or they don't.* She knocked her knuckle firmly on the table several times to get everyone's attention. They all looked up.

"Here's what we are going to do."

Chapter 20
South of Clonfert House
The Assault Begins

Major Lisset and her troop of women spirit warriors were about halfway to Clonfert House when one of her forward observers came rushing back to report that there were several witches in the eastern quarter. From what the observer could see, the witches were frantically looking for something or someone. Not soon after this observer arrived, one of her rear observers arrived with similar news. Witches were roaming the southern quarter on the hunt for something or someone.

"How many," Major Lisset asked each of them.

"Four in the east."

"Three in the south."

"Did they see you?"

"No, major," they responded. "I don't think so."

"Halt," the major called out to her women. "You two go back to your posts. If anything develops let me know immediately."

"Yes, major."

She said to her women, "let's take a brief rest."

Major Lisset withdrew beneath the branches of a nearby oak to be alone. She knew she had to notify the Headmaster, but there wasn't time to send a messenger. Should she risk sending him a thought message? Would the witches intercept it? She had no choice. She took the risk. She said to him in her thoughts, *"My women and I are on our way to you to help drive away the Sorcerer Corradhu. We are not far off. I must inform you that both my forward and rear observers have discovered witches roaming both the southern and eastern quarters. They are on the hunt for something. We thought you should know right away."*

Her message reached the Headmaster immediately. It also simultaneously reached Minda They both turned to Affey. The Headmaster called out her name. Minda and the Headmaster looked at each other. Minda spoke first.

"I just received a thought message from Major Lisset. Weird. Why did she send it to me?"

"I also received a message," the Headmaster said.

"About witches," Minda asked.

"Yes," he replied.

Affey turned to the Headmaster. "What did she say?"

Before he could answer Minda said, "It's the witches the Sorcerer Corradhu sent to look for Assunta."

Affey immediately instructed the Headmaster to tell Major Lisset that she had to go after the witches. "Please, tell Major Lisset that she must intercept these witches. Get them to surrender. Capture them by force if necessary. If they resist, then do what must be done to stop them."

Everyone in the Headmaster's study was caught off guard by Affey's resolve. She had just asked Major Lisset to stop the witches by any means necessary. Even death.

"Are you sure this is the right thing to do, Green Maiden," the Headmaster asked Affey. "This is a drastic step. It will only enflame the Sorcerer Corradhu."

"He's right," Professor O'Riley said.

Affey said calmly, "That can't be helped. Maybe if he gets even angrier it can be to our advantage. I hope it doesn't come to having to kill the witches. Hopefully, they will surrender. If not, then we must do what we must do."

"Very well, I'll tell her." The Headmaster sent the message to Major Lissett.

Affey asked Minda., "Has this ever happened to you before? Receiving a thought message?"

"Never. Why now?"

"Minda, your powers are growing." Affey was pleased to see her twin sister coming into her own. "This is will help us enormously."

"Affey. The Sorcerer Corradhu is heading back to his private encampment," Minda reported.

Affey put her hands on the table and took a deep breath then stood up straight.

"It's time to move, Kevin and Gianni. You must leave now. With any luck you can trap the Sorcerer Corradhu at his private encampment. Gianni, Kevin knows how. Trust him. More importantly, you must retrieve the sapphire staff and bring it here. You both know the risks. You will have to slay the nagas. If the Sorcerer Corradhu is there, the risks will be significantly greater. No matter what, you must secure the sapphire staff. Headmaster, can you please call on some of our spirit friends to convey them to the encampment? There is no time for them to go on foot."

"Of course," he said. He rang the bell on his desk. Several elves arrived to take Kevin and Gianni to face the nagas and maybe even the Sorcerer Corradhu. One of them brought Gianni's sword and dagger.

None of them knew it, but he had been training to become a master swordsman with Master Chan Wu for many years. He was so accomplished that Master Chan Wu had nothing more to teach Gianni. To celebrate Gianni's achievement at becoming a master, Master Chan Wu presented him with one of his ancestral swords, the Liu Doghen, the Dragon Slaying Sword. He also presented Gianni with a silver dagger. Turns out that, despite his affectations, Gianni was a warrior and a modest one at that. Kevin was impressed. Gianni must be some swordsman. They all agreed.

Before they left Affey gave each of them a hug. She said to Kevin, "be very careful. We, I, need you to come back." Kevin didn't say anything. "You can do this, Gianni," she said as she touched his swords as if blessing them. Neither Kevin nor Gianni responded.

As they were about to depart Minda saw that the Sorcerer Corradhu was turning away from his private encampment. He was headed back to the ritual clearing.

"He's heading back to the ritual clearing, Affey. Looks like he won't be at his private encampment when Kevin and Gianni arrive."

"Excellent," Affey said. "Please stay focused, Minda. Things are about to happen quickly." Affey turned her attention to Professor O'Riley who had remained uncharacteristically quiet.

"Professor, we need to set the defenses against the witches who are headed here. Can you do that?"

"Immediately," he said and left promptly to arrange for the defense of Clonfert House.

"Michael, do you know where the Sacred Fairy Scrolls are kept?"

"I do, why?"

"We need to hide them like Professor O'Riley did when Adena threatened them."

"I didn't go with him. I don't know where they should be taken. Why do we need to hide them? Are they threatened again?"

Affey said, "We just need to be safe. Can you do this or not?" She needed Michael to just do what she asked.

"Yes. I can call for the guardians," he said, not quite sure if he could or not. He didn't move.

"Now, Michael," the Headmaster said.

"Sorry. I'll go."

"Michael," Affey called out to him. "Somehow we will let you know when this is all over."

"That won't be necessary," he replied. "The guardians will know."

When Michael arrived at the Secret Library the guardians were there waiting for him. They escorted Michael and the Sacred Fairy Scrolls to Bronwyn's chapel where they remained safe once again.

The Headmaster, who had been sitting watching with amazement at Affey's command of the circumstances, asked her. "What about me, Green Maiden?"

"I need you to stay with me. I will need your counsel. I may need your powers. You should set additional guards around Assunta just in case the defenses are breached?"

"Consider it done." The Headmaster went to his study door and ordered one of his attendants to carry out Affey's orders.

Affey sat down. She closed her eyes for several minutes. She needed to do a quick assessment of where things stood before she made their next move. The Headmaster sat across from her waiting. Minda remained riveted on both the Sorcerer Corradhu at the ritual clearing and the nagas at his private encampments. Affey opened her eyes and stood up.

"It's time to go." The Headmaster stood up. He wasn't sure what he was supposed to do.

"Minda. Please come here," Affey called to her sister. Minda crossed the study to stand with her twin sister and the Headmaster.

"Minda. Can you continue Remote Viewing if we are on the move? Can you keep watching while we travel to the ritual clearing," Affey asked.

"I guess we're going to find out. I've never tried before."

A familiar voice called out to Affey from the study door. The Green Maiden entered with the help of the infirmarian.

"She insisted that I bring her here," the infirmarian said apologetically.

"I'll only take a minute Affey," the Green Maiden said as she directed the infirmarian to take her next to Affey. "I have something you will need."

Affey took the Green Maiden's hands to help steady her. The Green Maiden was nearing her end. Her emerald essence grew duller even as she stood there with Affey. The Green Maiden took a deep breath, placed her hands on Affey's cheeks and closed her eyes. A wave of energy ripped through Affey. The Green Maiden transferred another power to her. This power was magnitudes greater than the first one the Green Maiden transferred. They stood together, Affey eyes closed as well, the Green Maiden's hands on Affey's cheeks until the power stopped rippling through her was firmly embedded in Affey. The Green Maiden removed her hands from Affey's cheeks. She collapsed into the arms of the infirmarian.

"I better get her back."

"Please," Affey said to the infirmarian. They all watched as the Green Maiden left. None of them said it, but they all wondered if this would be the last time they saw her alive.

Affey knew exactly what power the Green Maiden transferred to her.

"We need to join hands in a circle," she said to the Headmaster and Minda. They followed her instructions. "I'm taking us to the ritual clearing."

Affey summoned her new power. She, Minda, and the Headmaster turned to vapor. She whisked them away to confront the Sorcerer Corradhu.

Chapter 21
Throughout the Realms
Pursuit of the Witches

Major Lisset dispatched two squadrons of six female spirits each to scour the east and southern quarters to capture the witches from the Sisters of the Coven. She chose them from the ranks of her Welsh fairies, the Tylwyth Teg. The reason she selected these women, is because their opponents always underestimated their prowess. The Tylwyth Teg were fair skinned with blonde hair. Their motto was, 'Death before Defeat'. Each carried a special sword forged with metal mined for them by the Knockers of the Dell. They also carried a ruby handled dagger engraved with the names of their ancestral heroines. They refused to wear any protective clothing, carry shields, or wear helmets. In battle, they were ferocious. The major thought they would carry out her orders swiftly and efficiently. She also thought they would return more witches dead than alive. She ordered each squadron to return with their captives, or their corpses, to Clonfert House as directed by Affey. Major Lisset and the rest of her women flew immediately to confront the witches headed to Clonfert House.

The squadron heading to the south encountered the three Sisters of the Coven as soon as they crossed the border into that quarter. The three Sisters did not see them at first. The squadron of Tylwyth Teg split up into teams of two to encircle the three witches without their knowing it. On a signal from the squadron leader, one team attacked the witches with flashes of violet light that momentarily blinded the witches. One of them, Julietta, let fly a shielding curse that dispersed the blinding light only to find the Tylwyth Teg were coming at them at high speed with their swords and daggers drawn. Fearing the worst, Julietta called out to the other two witches to head for cover in the forest. Unfortunately for them, the other team of Tylwyth Teg anticipated the direction of their flight and cut them off them. The other members of the squadron quickly joined them. Once surrounded, the three witches stood back-to-back in an effort to defend against the attack. One of them, Anna, lunged with her spear at the fairy nearest her, but the fairy dodged and slashed the witch's wrist. It was a deep wound. Anna dropped her spear and grabbed in her wrist in pain. The fairy took the spear and hurled it deep into the forest. The witch, Julietta, spoke out angrily.

"Who are you to assault us? We are Sisters of the Coven in service to the Sorcerer Corradhu. You are no match for us. Surrender and you will be spared the wrath of the Sorcerer Corradhu."

The Tylwyth Teg laughed so loud that their laughter echoed through the forest.

"Maybe we should introduce ourselves," the squadron leader said. "We are members of the spirit army of Major Lisset. We are the Tylwyth Teg. We don't care if you have heard of us or not. Nor do we cower at your supposed power. As for the Sorcerer Corradhu, his day is coming."

Another one of the witches, Philomena, reached for the sword on her belt.

"I wouldn't try that. You saw what happened to your sister when she tried to harm one of us. We won't hesitate to run your though," one of the Tylwyth Teg said with her hand on the ruby hilt of her dagger.

Unfortunately, Philomena didn't believe her. Philomena withdrew her sword and swung it in a circle at the fairies. No matter how hard she tried, they could parry every one of her swings or thrusts. She continued for several minutes until her arm grew so tired that she could barely hold it up any longer.

"Have you had enough now? Put down your sword before we have to take it from you," another one of the Tylwyth Teg said.

Philomena struggled to raise her sword one more time, but as soon as it was in a striking position, her strength failed. She dropped it. One of the Tylwyth Teg swooped in to take it. This left only one witch, Julietta, who had not tried to attack. She dropped her sword and dagger on the ground. She said to the fairy women, "you do not understand. We must fight you even to the death or the Sorcerer Corradhu will deal with us very harshly."

The squadron leader picked up Julietta's sword and dagger and handed them to one of the other women. The three witches stood together trying to be defiant. They were not convincing.

"There is a way for you to save yourselves. Surrender to us. We will take you to our major at Clonfert House. There, you will tell her everything you know about the Sorcerer Corradhu and his intentions. Your other choice is to remain silent. Make that choice and the Sorcerer Corradhu's punishment will pale in comparison. Which will it be?"

The witch Julietta asked, "may we have a minute to ourselves to decide?"

"Of course. Be quick about it." The squadron leader said. She gestured for the Tylwyth Teg to take a few steps back from the witches.

Once they were out of earshot, Julietta said to the witches, "we cannot surrender. If we pretend to, then maybe once we are close enough to them, we can grab their swords and kill them all. What other choice do we have?"

Philomena strongly disagreed. "There are six of them. We are three with no weapons. You saw what they can do. We are no match for them."

Anna, whose wrist was bleeding badly, also disagreed. "I cannot attack with my wrist like this."

Julietta was not persuaded. "I will cast a blinding spell on them. In their confusion we can take their weapons and kill them. The Sorcerer Corradhu will be pleased when we bring back their bodies."

Again, Anna disagreed. "He will only be pleased if we bring back Assunta. Maybe we should just go with them. If Assunta is with them, then we might have a chance to take her."

Julietta would not be deterred. "I am casting the blinding spell. Either you help me, or you don't."

She didn't wait for an answer. She turned toward the Tylwyth Teg, raised her right hand, and began by saying, "I summon..." That was all she said. One of the Tylwyth Teg, suspecting it was the start of some spell, cut off her arm. Philomena crumbled to the grounds in agony. Another one of the fairies rushed to her and bound her arm to stop the bleeding. "Don't," the squadron leader ordered. "She had her chance. Leave her here."

"Bind these two!" the squadron leader ordered. "We are taking them to the Major at Clonfert House."

"You'll regret this," Julietta cried out.

The Tylwyth Teg ignored her. Shortly after they departed Julietta succumbed from the loss of blood from her severed arm.

Meanwhile, the squadron of Tylwyth Teg in the eastern quarter was not having as much luck. When they first surveyed the eastern quarter, they couldn't locate a single witch. They didn't know that the witches in this quarter had split up. Frustrated in their attempts to find the witches, they also split into teams of two. They took off in different directions searching for the witches. This time they were successful, though their success did not come easily.

One of the teams discovered the witch, Patrice, tormenting a family of Brownies. As the fairies swooped in to rescue them, Patrice sensed their approach, but didn't immediately turn to challenge them. She waited until they were almost upon her then she turned around furiously swinging her sword in a wide arc. It struck one of the Tylwyth Teg who fell to the ground with a fatal wound.

The other Tylwyth Teg, one of Major Lisset's most accomplished combatants, soared high into the sky daring the witch to follow her. Patrice didn't hesitate. She pursued the fairy high above the forest canopy. The fairy swooshed and swirled through the branches of the trees finding small passages that would be difficult for the witch to navigate. When Patrice attempted to follow the Tylwyth Teg through an especially small opening, the witch became entangled in some ivy. Seeing that the witch was trapped, the Tylwyth Teg flew back, her sword and dagger drawn. The witch attempted to reach for dagger, but when she did, she dropped her sword. She looked up to see the fast-approaching fairy, She dropped her dagger. She was defenseless unless she could cast a spell to thwart the Tylwyth Teg. She needed to use both of her hands to direct the spell, but one of them was caught in the ivy. She struggled to free it. The Tylwyth Teg knew what Patrice was trying to do, so she flew behind the witch where she was certain the witch could not see her or throw the spell in her direction.

"Witch," the fairy said, "its best that you surrender. You cannot cast a spell in your current circumstances. Surrender to me and I will free you from these branches. Otherwise, I will lash you to this tree where you will eventually perish."

"You don't scare me, fairy. Go ahead, leave me here. My other sisters will return soon to rescue me. Then, the four of us will pursue you and your kind to the ends of the earth. When we are finished, the world will be rid of you spirits."

The witch revealed some alarming news. First, there were four witches roaming the eastern quarter. Second, she revealed the Sorcerer Corradhu's intentions. He was not going to stop with the Western Quarter. He had his eyes on all fairydom. This information had to get back the major quickly. The Tylwyth Teg was done talking.

"I will ask you one last time, witch. Surrender of you will leave me no choice."

"Never," the witch Patrice yelled as loud as she could. She hoped her scream would reach the other sisters and they would rush back.

The Tylwyth Teg knew that the witch was calling out to her sisters. She had to act.

"So be it." The Tylwyth Teg flew fast and hard toward the witch Patrice. Her sword pierced the witch's heart, dispatching her with a single thrust. The fairy left the dead witch dangling in the branches as a warning should the other witches come. She flew frantically through the Eastern Quarter looking for the other members of her squadron. She found them in a tense confrontation with two of the witches. This meant one was still at large.

When they all saw the Tylwyth Teg approaching they momentarily stopped.

"Why are you alone," one of the Tylwyth Teg asked.

"One of our sisters is dead." This enflamed the Tylwyth Teg,

"So, now there are three for us to slay," one of the witches called out taunting the fairies.

The Tylwyth Teg who just returned from killing the witch Patrice taunted them back. "Well, at least there is one less of you." This changed the witches' tone.

"What do you mean," one of them asked.

She said, "surrender to us or you will find out." This enraged the witches.

They raised their swords together to the sky. A single bolt of lightning rose from the tips of their swords spilling across the sky above them. No sooner did the sky light up, than a dark, thunderous cloud overtook it. A voice spoke from a direction none of them could determine.

"There will be none of that here, witches." A blanket of fog rolled low across the ground. Not far from them a small, ancient man in a tattered overcoat approached accompanied by a nymph. "Here, in this realm, there is no place for spells, curses, charms, and the like. Spirit confronts spirit in the traditional ways. Your spells are forever blocked here." The cloud overhead dispersed. The witches tried again to throw the lightning bolt, but they failed.

"Heed my words, all of you. That includes Tylwyth Teg as well. No magic among you." With that the ancient man vanished into the air.

One of the witches saw this as an opportunity to attack. The Tylwyth Teg, being smaller and nimbler than the witches, out maneuvered them. They grouped together to await the witches' next move.

"I will ask you witches again, surrender or else." The squadron leader said.

The witches attacked.

The Tylwyth Teg spilt up and drew the three witches apart so they could not attack as one. It didn't take long for them to prevail. The first witch to succumb was Theresa. When she tried to strike, one of the Tylwyth Teg threw her dagger with such force that it went right through the witch, killing her instantly. The witch, Magdalena, attacked with a fury none of the Tylwyth Teg had ever encountered. Before she was felled, she struck one of the fairies so hard that it landed unconscious several hundred yards away. As the witch, Magdalena, turned to see where the Tylewyth Teg landed, two of the others attacked. They disarmed her causing only minor injuries. They quickly bound her in chains to a nearby tree. In so doing, they lost sight of the witch, Monica.

Fearing for her own life and desperate to inform the Sorcerer Corradhu of all that had happened, the witch, Monica, fled back to the ritual clearing ground in the Western Quarter.

"She fled," one of the Tylwyth Teg said as she looked around for the witch, Monica.

"Let her go. We need to take this one back to the Major." They yanked the bound witch to her feet. They flew her toward Clonfert House and Major Lisset.

The witch Monica reported everything to the Sorcerer Corradhu. If her assessment was correct, thought the Sorcerer Corradhu, the witches headed to Clonfert House may encounter the same fate. Perhaps he should recall them to shore up the defenses of the ritual clearing.

"Monica. You are to go immediately toward Clonfert House. Find your sisters. Tell them to return immediately. I believe the spirits will move against us. I want to draw them into the ritual clearing ground where my power is strongest. We will defeat them here."

The witch, Monica, flew with all speed toward Clonfert House. Just as the silhouette of Clonfert House appeared on the horizon, she saw several bodies on the ground below her. Even though she was flying high above the ground, these bodies looked familiar. She swooped down to discover the bodies of two sisters of the coven. This meant that only one of the sisters headed to Clonfert may have survived.

Of the Eleven Sisters of the Coven, only three remained alive. Monica herself, Magdalena who was taken away in chains, and Assunta who had betrayed them all.

Seeing the carnage below her, the witch, Monica, knew there was no point in going any further. The Sorcerer Corradhu must be informed of how bad things had become. Monica hesitated for only a minute. "Should I go to Clonfert House and surrender? At least I would be alive. No. I will not betray my lineage or the Sorcerer Corradhu." She returned to the ritual clearing to find it empty. Where was the Sorcerer Corradhu?

As his paced the ritual clearing waiting for the witches to return with news of Assunta, the Sorcerer Corradhu saw a bright flash of energy burst over the eastern sky. The Sisters of the Coven whom he sent there were engaged in a confrontation. There is no other reason why they would summon that amount of energy. Rather than wait for their return, he twirled rapidly becoming no more than a hint of a breeze. He went in the direction of the flash of energy.

In an instant, he was able to fly over the southern and eastern quarters. What he saw was not what he expected. One witch was dead, one badly wounded, one in chains, and one, at least, was missing. The witch in chains was surrounded by several female spirits. He could tell that they were warriors of some kind from their weapons. They had dealt the sisters a terrible defeat. Who were these spirits? Why had they challenged his witches? The only conclusion he could reach was that they were hunting the witches. This could only mean that Assunta told them his plans. Where were these spirits keeping her? Rather than challenging them, he decided to remain drifting as a mist on the air, following them a short distance behind. They were headed north, in the direction of Clonfert House. That is where he would find Assunta. He wondered if the Sisters of the Coven he sent there were having any luck finding her.

It wasn't long before the Tylwyth Teg together with their captive witch were near to Clonfert House. When the Sorcerer Corradhu saw the bodies of several of witches on the ground below him, he was confused. How could this be? What power or magic slew these witches? This was an ominous sign. Since they seemed to know quite a lot about the activities of the witches, he wondered how much they knew about him. He turned back to go first to his private encampment to grab his sapphire staff. He didn't want to be without it any longer. He reached for the pouch of the Sacred Soil of the Su Nuraxi, but it was not on his belt. He had to return to the ritual clearing, the seat of all of his power. He was certain these fairies, whoever they are, were coming for him.

Chapter 22
The Sorcerer Corradhu's Private Encampment The Fight for the Sapphire Staff

Just before Kevin and Gianni arrived at the Sorcerer Corradhu's private encampment Gianni suggested that their fairy escorts drop them along the edge of the encampment. There, they could remain hidden while they surveyed the area. Since neither of them knew anything about the private encampment, Gianni suggested they proceed cautiously. The fairies did as they were asked. They set Kevin and Gianni down in a thick patch of brush from where they could see the entirety of the Sorcerer Corradhu's private encampment.

The first thing Kevin noticed was how similar it was to the place the Headmaster took him to practice. He whispered to Gianni.

"This is exactly like the clearing the Headmaster took me to practice. If I didn't know I was somewhere else, I would swear I was in the same place."

"Then it should make your job easy. Easier than mine, I'm afraid," Gianni said pointing to the center of the encampment.

"Oh," Kevin said putting his hand up to his mouth. "Are those the nagas? They are much bigger than I expected. They look nasty."

The nagas, who had been napping with their heads resting on the ground between their front claws, raised their heads sharply and turned in the direction of Kevin and Gianni. Gianni grabbed Kevin by the arm and pulled him down behind the brush.

"Don't move or make a sound."

Gianni used one hand to gently push aside one of the limbs of the bush in front of him to see what the nagas were doing.

They were sitting up on their haunches, their heads turned skyward, sniffing at the air. Gianni noticed that they were fastened to two massive granite blocks with heavy chains. He saw the sapphire staff imbedded in another equally massive block of granite between the two nagas, just as Minda described. He said to Kevin, "This is going to be much more difficult that I thought. Look." He motioned for Kevin to look through the same small opening Gianni made in the bush.

"This is impossible. Even if I can trap them under my inescapable dome and within the impenetrable walls, then how will you ever be able to get the sapphire staff. You will never get passed those creatures. We need to go back and tell Affey we can't do this." Kevin started to stand up. When Gianni pulled him back down Kevin stumbled and fell. It made enough noise to draw the nagas' attention. Gianni peeked over the bush. He didn't like what he saw.

"Even if we wanted to leave, there is no chance of that now."

"Why," Kevin asked. He was more scared than he had ever been in his life.

"Take another look," Gianni said.

Kevin kneeled up next to Gianni to look over the bush. The nagas knew where they were. They must have either smelled them or heard them. Now, they saw them. It didn't matter which. The nagas were snarling and spitting. They were straining with all their might at their chains. Kevin was sure the chains would snap at any minute and the nagas would be upon them before they could run away. Gianni had a different reaction. When faced with danger, Gianni's courage inspired others. Kevin had no idea just how brave Gianni was.

"They have seen us. We made a promise to Affey to get that sapphire staff and we are going to get it. Those chains are strong enough to hold them. The Sorcerer Corradhu is not so stupid as to let those nagas run loose. I suspect they would even attack him if they wanted to."

"Are you out of your mind, Gianni? Those things can't be taken down. Come on, let's get out of here."

Gianni had had enough. He slapped Kevin hard enough that the crack of his hand on Kevin's cheek reverberated through the encampment. The nagas stopped their snarling and gnashing.

"Weave that damn dome and raise the walls, Kevin." Gianni stood up and drew the Liu Doghen, the Dragon Slaying Sword, from its sheath. He released the silver dagger from his belt. He stepped out from behind the bushes. This set the nagas to screeching and howling. They pawed at the ground. Foam dropped from their mouths. The iron collars around their necks dug into their flesh so hard they were starting to bleed. Kevin was afraid they were going to break free and devour Gianni.

"What are you waiting for Kevin. Set the dome. We can't afford to have the sorcerer or any of his witches show up now. I can handle this as long as these nagas don't have help." Gianni began to move slowly toward the nagas.

Kevin cowered behind the push. He heard a voice. It was the Ancient Man. "Get up, Kevin. Gianni is exposed. If you don't set the inescapable dome and raise the walls he will die. It will be your fault. Now, get up. Remember what I told you. Confidence. I have it in you. You have it in yourself. Now, get up."

What Kevin did next was completely unexpected not just by Gianni, but by Kevin himself.

Kevin stood up as tall as he could. He pushed through the brush and walked straight toward the nagas.

"What are you doing," Gianni yelled.

Kevin ignored him. He continued walking toward the nagas who were getting more agitated. Kevin stopped just far enough away from the nagas that, no matter how they stretched their necks, pulled at their chains, or reached for him with their talons, he remained just beyond their reach. The spit from their foul mouths hit him in the face, Kevin stared at them. Then, he raised his arms to the trees.

The branches began to sway. They grew longer and longer as Kevin wove them into an intricate, inescapable dome. The bushes and brush on the forest floor rose like fortress walls to mingle with the overarching branches. The nagas stood still watching the forest grow thicker and thicker. Kevin sensed they were afraid.

Gianni, who wanted to watch what Kevin was doing because he had never seen anything like it before, knew that he had to attack the nagas now while they were distracted by Kevin. For his part, was getting close to finishing the inescapable dome and walls. He checked on Gianni. Gianni had somehow managed to circle behind the nagas. They did not seem to see him approaching. Kevin worried that if he finished too soon, the nagas would no longer be interested in him. They would turn on Gianni. Out of nowhere, Kevin commanded the limbs, branches, bush, and leaves to make noise. He directed them to make as haunting a sound as possible. Kevin didn't know where this idea came from, but he hoped it would provide enough cover for Gianni to attack and sever the nagas' tails.

Gianni crept up behind the nagas. Neither one of the them seem to be aware of his approach. When he was within striking distance, he swung the Liu Doghen, The Dragon Slaying Sword, with all his might. It cutoff one of the Nagas's tails. The Naga fell dead to the ground. The other Naga snapped around so quickly that it bit Gianni on his sword wielding arm. Though the pain was nearly unbearable, Gianni held fast to his sword. Before he scooted back out of reach of the Naga, he was able to embed his silver dagger under its chin. This appeared to weaken the Naga, but not stop it. What Gianni didn't anticipate was that the severed tail from the dead Naga would take on a life of its own. He had not been warned about this. None of them had.

The Nagas's tail flew erratically around the encampment. Kevin was able to duck out of its way several times. The severed tail seemed to be looking for Gianni. At one point, the severed tail fell to the ground. Gianni, struggling to raise his sword, ran toward the tail to put it down once and for all. But just as he was about to plunge the sword into it, the severed tail coiled and lashed Gianni across the chest. Gianni fell on his back. The Liu Doghen, the Dragon Slaying Sword, had fallen from his hand just out of reach. He had no weapon. The severed tail, now looking more like a coiled cobra about to strike, hissed over Gianni, tormenting him. Gianni was defenseless.

Seeing what was happening to Gianni, Kevin reached in his pocket. One thing he had done, which none of the others did, was always carry with him the disc Master Chan Wu gave them when they first came to Clonfert House. The master told them that if they were ever in a dangerous situation they could not escape, all they had to do was press the disc and the master would come to rescue them. Professor O'Riley made modifications so it would work in this realm. If there was ever a time to us the disc, this was it. He hoped the modifications world work.

Kevin pulled out the disc and pressed it as hard as he could. It emitted such a loud, high pitch sound that it stunned the severed tail. It dropped to the ground writhing in pain. Gianni grabbed the Liu Doghen, the Dragon Slaying Sword, and hacked the severed tail into several pieces putting an end to it. This caused such rage in the other Naga that it ripped its chain from the granite block. It rushed at Gianni. Kevin wanted to help, but didn't know what more to do.

"I don't know what to do, Gianni. I have to keep the dome sealed."

"Do what you have to do, Kevin."

Kevin realized that, even though he called for Master Chan Wu to rescue them, he wouldn't be able to penetrate the dome. Kevin underestimated the master.

"Get out of my way, Mister O'Connell." It was Master Chan Wu. He shoved Kevin back. The Naga heard the master's voice. It turned on him. As it did, Gianni swung at its tail, but missed. The Naga snapped back at Gianni. When it did, the master cut of its tail with one swift stroke of his sword. The Naga fell to the ground dead. Gianni collapsed to the ground exhausted. He was wounded, but he would heal. As soon as the Nagas's tail was sliced off, Kevin ran and withdrew the sapphire staff from the granite block. It was the last heroic thing he would do.

Master Chan Wu turned around to tell Kevin to release the dome when he saw what Kevin had done. Kevin laid on the ground clutching the sapphire staff to his chest. The severed tail of the Naga draped over him. The sharp end of the tail pierced Kevin's heart. The Naga was dead. Kevin was dead.

Gianni and Master Chan Wu ran to Kevin, but there was nothing they could do.

"He should not have died like this, Master Chan Wu," Gianni said through his tears.

"We die when we die, Mister Giannotti. You should know that. It was Kevin's time. His death will not be in vain. His is a hero's death. We must both mourn him and honor him. It is what is right." Master Chan Wu reached down, took the sapphire staff, and handed it to Gianni. "Take this to Affey."

"What about Kevin," Gianni asked concerned that the master was going to leave Kevin's body behind.

"I will carry Kevin back. Come. It's time to leave this cursed place."

Master Chan Wu picked Kevin up into his arms. He uttered a prayer under his breath for Kevin's rebirth in a better world. Then, he and Gianni vanished. They would reappear at Clonfert House in an instant.

Chapter 23
The Sorcerer Corradhu

Affey delivered the three of them, Minda, the Headmaster, and herself to the fringe of the sorcerer's ritual clearing. Affey thought it best for them to arrive undetected, if at all possible. No sooner had they materialized in the forest than Minda spoke with urgency.

"Affey, I lost contact with Kevin, Gianni, and the Sorcerer Corradhu as soon as you shifted us into our ethereal forms. When I'm not my usual human self, it seems I lose my ability to Remote View."

The Headmaster interjected. "I should have seen this coming, Minda. Affey, I am sorry that I failed you in this."

"Can you see them now," Affey asked.

"I'm trying. My view is from above the inescapable dome Kevin has woven. I can't seem to penetrate through it."

Affey was troubled by this development. She didn't want Kevin and Gianni left without the possibility of rescue if something went wrong. "Can you find the Sorcerer Corradhu? Is he there?"

Minda gathered every ounce of power she could muster, but she simply could not get through the dome. She cast her remote viewing over the nearby woods outside the dome and saw the Sorcerer Corradhu approaching.

"I have him. He's getting very near to his private encampment. He keeps fading in and out of my view. I think it has to do with the dome. The closer he is getting the fuzzier my vision is."

"Stay with him, Minda. Headmaster, stay here with Minda. I'm going to move closer to the ritual clearing to see who is there. Let me know if anything happens at the private encampment."

Affey moved Minda and the Headmaster deeper into the shadowy cover of the forest. She wanted them to remain hidden as long as possible.

It came as somewhat of a surprise to Affey when she saw that only a single witch was present at the ritual clearing. Where we the others? Has Major Lissot had some success? The lone witch paced back and forth in front of the altar wringing her hands. Affey was convinced that something was very wrong. She returned to Minda and the Headmaster to find out what Minda had seen.

He was about a hundred yards from the entrance to his private encampment when the Sorcerer Corradhu noticed that something about the forest was not right. It looked as though the trees, bushes, and scrubs had grown thicker, taller in the brief time he had been away. Usually from this vantage point he could see clearly into his private encampment. He should be able to see the nagas curled up, ready to strike any intruder. Now, all he saw was dense growth. It was so thick he couldn't see but a few feet through it. He as certain the pathway into his private encampment should be right in front of him, but there was no trace of it. Had he been confused about where he was? *Certainly not*, he thought.

He quickened his steps. At the spot where the pathway should have been, the sorcerer encountered such a thick, intertwined thicket of brambles that he could not go any further. He ran several yards to his left looking for any way through Everywhere he turned he faced an impenetrable tangle of forest growth. Frustrated, he began to tear at the vegetation. The more he ripped and tore it, the thicker it got. He ran to another spot and tried again. It was the same. He could not get through. He had nothing with which to try to cut away the forest. He never carried a sword or knife because he didn't need to. His powers were always enough. The Sorcerer Corradhu stepped back away from the tangle of forest. He calmed himself down. Looking upward to the sky, he called out, "Come all you birds and beast of the woodlands. It is I, your sorcerer and master, who command it." He would command them to peck and chew a way through.

Nothing. Not a single bird or beast arrived. The Sorcerer Corradhu started to panic. He screamed, "I command it."

Again, nothing. He ran straight at the tangle of forest again. He tied once more to tear his way through it. His hands were bloody from the thorns. His face was badly scratched. His robes torn. His hair, always so beautiful, was twisted in knots like the forest itself.

"I will destroy whoever is responsible for this magic. I am the Sorcerer Corradhu. I will spare you no torment."

He let a bolt of lightning flow from his right hand. He was going to force it through the forest wall and use it as a lasso to pull out his sapphire staff. Everything crackled with his power. All, that is, except the inescapable dome. The lightning bolt was blocked.

"I will have my sapphire staff. Bring it to me now." Again, he threw a bolt directly at the forest wall in front of him. The bolt of lightning shivered up the forest wall and disappeared into the sky above. At that moment he heard one of the nagas cry out painfully. Then he heard a second cry. Then everything went still and quiet. The forest wall began to fade. The pathway into his private encampment opened. He rushed down the pathway, his torn robes and disheveled hair tailing behind him. When he saw the nagas dead bodies, their tails severed, he screamed out with a mix of pain and rage. Then he saw it was gone. His sapphire staff was no longer embedded in the granite block. The Sorcerer Corradhu ran to his private quarters looking for the Sacred Soil of the Su Nuraxi. He forgot that he lost it on the ritual clearing grounds. He was in a state of panic.

"They took the soil? How dare they. I will torture them. Kill them. Toss their bodies to the four corners of the earth."

The Sorcerer Corradhu flew up into the sky. He threw bolts of thunder and lightning in spirals of power in all directions. "I am coming for you," he yelled. "Meet me at my ritual clearing ground, if you dare." He let loose another round of his power and flew to his ritual clearing ground.

Minda wanted to call out to Affey to tell her that she had seen everything that happened to the Sorcerer Corradhu, but she feared that if she did, she would give them away. Instead, she asked the Headmaster, "can you communicate with Affey? The Sorcerer Corradhu is on his was here and he is livid."

"Yes, I can warn her. Anything else?"

"Yes. Tell her the nagas are dead and the sapphire staff is not there. Neither are Kevin and Gianni."

"Kevin and Gianni did it," the Headmaster said too loudly. The witch Monica heard him. She turned in his direction.

Affey also heard him, but she also heard his thought message that the Sorcerer Corradhu was on his way there. The witch Monica was moving purposely toward where Affey was hiding, but she didn't think the witch knew she was there. The witch Monica was searching for the place from where she heard the voice. When she was very close to Affey, close enough that if she wasn't looking in the distance for where the voice came from, she would have seen Affey, Affey stood up suddenly in front of her. The witch, Monica, nearly feel over backward with surprise.

"Who are you to dare intrude on his hallowed ground," the witch, Monica, demanded.

Affey didn't immediately respond. Instead, she stepped in closer to the witch, Monica. The witch stood her ground.

"I will give you but one chance to surrender to me witch, or..." Affey started to say before the witch interrupted her.

"Or what, fairy? You think your fairy spells can harm me? You have no idea of the power I wield. I will hold you captive until my master, the Sorcerer Corradhu, arrives. He will deal with you in ways you will not be able to handle." The witch Monica raised her arm to cast a spell at Affey.

Affey remained perfectly still. The spell had no effect. The witch, Monica, tried another spell, and then another. Each time she became more and more anxious about her failure to subdue Affey. Affey had had enough of the witch.

"I told you, witch, you had one chance to surrender. You did not. Now your fate is cast." Affey spread both her arms wide. She brought her palms together over her head. When she did, the wind blew around the witch like a tornado. It lifted her off the ground.

"You will be bound to this earth forever, witch."

Botsam, accompanied by two of the other guardians of the Eo Mugna, arrived.

"Bind her to the roots of the Eo Mugna Tree," she ordered. Her finals words to the witch, Monica, were, "your evil will be taken form you forever. You will writhe in horrible pain as you are intertwined with the roots of my sacred tree. Farwell, witch. Your kind will no longer wander here."

Fighting against the restraints Botsam placed on her, the witch, Monica, yelled out as she was hauled off, "the Sorcerer Corradhu will slay you. Then he will come to your damned Eo Mugna Tree, cut it down, and rescue me."

Affey waived her hand angrily at the witch, Monica. It sealed her mouth shut, never to utter a sound again.

Minda and the Headmaster watched from inside the shadows of the forest. The Headmaster was shaken by Affey's display of power. He had no idea that a Green Maiden could harbor such resolute actions. Affey, the new Green Maiden, was more powerful than any other Green Maiden. No one could defeat her.

Minda didn't know whether to be proud of her twin sister, the Green Maiden, or to be terrified of her. This Green Maiden was not her timid, cautious twin sister. Affey, the Green Maiden, was fearsome. How would she deal with Affey? Could you have sisterly affection for a creature that could so easily dispatch a witch to eternal torment? Could she be a sister to a creature who could, with the wave of a hand, seal her mouth shut? Minda was sad and scared. She was so caught up in her emotions that she failed to see the arrival of the Sorcerer Corradhu. Affey, however, felt him coming. The scent of his anger arrived before he did. She could smell it. It fed her resolve to defeat him. She stood at his altar in the very spot where her performed the ritual for the curse. The Headmaster stayed hidden.

The Sorcerer Corradhu stopped abruptly in the sky above the ritual clearing. He saw Affey, the Green Maiden, standing defiantly at his altar. He immediately caused a gale force wind to sweep across the ritual clearing. It tore limbs from the branches, uprooted trees. The wind ripped through the encircling forest causing havoc. It kicked up so much dust and debris that the entire ritual cleaning ground was hidden from the sorcerer's view. He disbursed the winds. He ordered calm restored. When the dust cleared, he fully expected Affey, the Green Maiden, to be have been crushed under a tree. To his shock, there Affey, the Green Maiden, stood at the altar as if nothing had happened. The Sorcerer Corradhu slowly descended from the sky. Affey, the Green Maide watched his every move.

"So, it is a Green Maiden who dares to challenge me. And you are young one as well." While he spoke, he floated around close to her. Affey didn't flinch.

"On whose account do you set foot on my ritual cleaning ground? Surely, you must know what happens here, or else you would not have come." He moved to face her head on. "You will tell me and tell me now, Green Maiden, should you wish to have any chance of surviving." The Sorcerer Corradhu

164

snapped his head toward several trees that had fallen at the edge of the clearing. There was movement there.

"Come out and identify yourself," he said.

"Stay where you are," Affey, the Green Maiden, called out to Minda and the Headmaster.

The Sorcerer Corradhu turned to Affey with a sardonic snicker. "How many of you are there that I can destroy? Ignore this Green Maiden," he called out to them. "You answer to me now."

The Headmaster stepped out into view.

"YOU," the Sorcerer Corradhu said through is gnashing teeth. "I thought I was rid of you."

"Apparently not," the Headmaster said as he walked toward the sorcerer.

The Sorcerer Corradhu let fly a flash of energy that the Headmaster easily deflected. Affey, the Green Maiden, started to raise her hand to defend the Headmaster.

"Do not move Green Maiden or I will slay him in an instant," the sorcerer warned her.

The Headmaster said, "leave him to me, Green Maiden." The Headmaster continued to advance.

"Yes, Headmaster, come closer. I want this Green Maiden to watch your soul depart from this world," the sorcerer said as he started to walk toward the Headmaster.

Affey, the Green Maiden, tried to communicate with her thoughts to Minda, but she couldn't. She didn't know that Minda laid unconscious under a heavy branch that fell on her.

The Headmaster and the Sorcerer Corradhu continued to advance on each other. Affey, the Green Maiden, was not sure when she should intervene, but intervene she would. The Headmaster could not carry the fight to the Sorcerer Corradhu. Had he forgotten the prophecy in all the chaos and confusion? Affey thought, *I will use this posturing between the two of them to move in and strike the Sorcerer Corradhu.* This is exactly what she did.

The two magicians, one human and one witch, hurled insults and spells at each other. Neither one seemed to get the upper hand. Affey, the Green Maiden, watched the sorcerer carefully for any sign of vulnerability. She noticed that he preferred to circle to his right. Whenever he was forced to move left, he found a way to dodge and bring the fight back to his preferred position.

She also noticed that when he did this, he momentarily dropped his left arm leaving his chest exposed. A strike there at the right moment could stop his heart. He would drop dead instantly. She waited for the Sorcerer Corradhu's strength to ebb. His energy would have to slow given how ferociously he and the Headmaster went at each other. The sorcerer was being forced left by the Headmaster. Affey, the Green Maiden, prepared to make her move.

She held and held and held. Then, just as she was sure the sorcerer was going to force a shift in the action, he hurled a spell at the Headmaster that blew him to the edge of the cleaning. The Headmaster fell with a terrible thud against a tree trunk. Affey, the Green Maiden, thought it might have killed him. The Sorcerer Corradhu was racing to finish off the Headmaster. She could wait no longer.

Affey, the Green Maiden, reached down and picked up the dagger the witch Monica left behind at the foot of the altar. She flew with all speed with the dagger in her outstretched hand toward the Sorcerer Corradhu. She reached him just as he was about to unleash his final spell on the Headmaster. Sensing her approach, the Sorcerer Corradhu turned around to strike. He was too late. Affey swooped low under his left arm and thrust the dagger into his chest. She twisted it hard. She could feel his ribs splinter as she turned it in his chest. The sorcerer grabbed at his chest in pain. He caught Affey's hand and squeezed it, trying to work it free from the blade. He looked at her with eyes aflame. Affey, the Green Maiden, was about to remove the dagger and thrust it once again into his chest when the Headmaster let out a cry of excruciating pain. It distracted Affey, the Green Maiden, for just a second. It was long enough for the Sorcerer Corradhu to push her away. He flew fast and high above the broken trees. He pulled the dagger from his chest and hurled in down at her. The dagger landed point first on the altar. It seeped the sorcerer's blood from its blade across the granite. Affey, the Green Maiden, flew to the Headmaster. He needed her more than she needed to go after the sorcerer.

From high above them the Sorcerer Corradhu yelled, "this is not the end of us Green Maiden. I will have my revenge," When the Sorcerer Corradhu said the word 'revenge' he too screamed in pain as he clutched his chest. He gave one last hateful look and disappeared over the trees. Where he went would remain a mystery.

Affey heard stirring in the underbrush. Minda sat up, her hair full of twigs. Her face had some serious scratches. There were trickles on blood on her cheeks. "Are you okay, Minda?" Affey, the Green Maiden, asked from where she was attending to the Headmaster.

"I think so, Affey. Nothing seems to be broken."

"Help me with the Headmaster. He's badly hurt. We need to get him back to Clonfert House."

"What about the Sorcerer Corradhu? Should you go after him?"

"He's badly wounded. I don't think he'll make it very far. We've done what we needed to do. It's time for us all to go home."

A small voice came from the direction of the altar. It was singing a pleasant tune.

Minda, despite her injuries, cast her Remote View toward the altar. "There are spirits trapped underneath the altar."

"I'll release them," Affey, the Green Maiden said. She pulled the locked chest from underneath the altar. One by one she released the spirits from their cages. They thanked her and took off to their homes to spread the news that the Sorcerer Corradhu was defeated. The last spirit to be released was the leprechaun.

"Oh, you are the Green Maiden. I've always wanted to meet you. Here, I have something for you." She held out the pouch with the Sacred Soil of the Su Nuraxi.

"Thank you, miss. I know what this is. I pray I will never need it."

The leprechaun gave a slight nod of her head and took off to the north.

Affey, the Green Maiden, went back to Minda and the Headmaster. She reached out her hand for Minda's hand to help her up. They each took one of the Headmaster's hands. Affey, the Green Maiden, transformed them into a whisp of air to carry them back to Clonfert House. Little did they know the sadness they would find there.

Chapter 24
Clonfert House
Funeral Rites

Affey, the Green Maiden, transported the Headmaster directly to the infirmary. When all three of them materialized in the triage area, they were met by a young physician, Doctor Nimesh, He was in a somber mood. Minda explained that the Headmaster had taken a serious fall and hit his head against a tree. She didn't even attempt to explain the circumstances. The young doctor performed a quick assessment.

"He has a concussion. Until we examine him more closely, I cannot tell you how serious it is."

The Headmaster was fighting to keep his eyes open. He knew sleeping would not be a good thing for him. The doctor called for the infirmarian.

"Take the Headmaster to my examination room. Keep him awake. Start an IV and schedule a CAT scan."

"Yes, doctor." The infirmarian helped settle the Headmaster on a gurney then wheeled him down the hallway. The doctor pulled Affey, the Green Maiden, and Minda aside.

"I know who you are Minda, but I'm afraid I do not know you, madam fairy." The doctor was skeptical of Affey, the Green Maiden.

She explained. "I was once a student here, but as you can see, I am no longer who I was then. I am the new Green Maiden."

"I'm a new doctor here having once been a student myself. Forgive me, but I know nothing about the Green Maiden."

Minda said to the doctor. "Doctor, this Green Maiden is my twin sister. She and I were instrumental in the defeat of Adena. You may have heard about that."

"I have," replied the doctor. "So, you are the Temne twins?"

"We are. But as you can see, my sister, Affey, is now of another realm."

Affey, the Green Maiden, saw sadness in the doctor's eyes. Minda did not see it. She asked the doctor, "what is troubling you, doctor? I can see it in your eyes."

The young doctor hesitated. He wasn't sure if he was authorized to tell them the reason why. "I suppose it is alright if I tell you since you came in with the Headmaster. One of the students who went out on an assignment from him met with the end of his life. His companion, was also hurt, but his injuries are not life threatening."

Minda sat down on the floor with her head in her hands. Affey, the Green Maiden asked, "is it a junior or senior student who has died?"

"A junior. I believe his name is Kevin O'Connell."

Affey, the Green Maiden, couldn't hold back her tears. She dropped to the floor next to Minda. The two sisters held each other and wept. The young doctor, unsure how to comfort them, left to attend to the Headmaster.

It took Affey, the Green Maiden, and her twin sister, Minda several minutes to collect themselves. "We have to find Professor O'Riley." Affey, the Green Maiden said as she helped her sister up. Together they went to the professor's study.

Professor O'Riley's door was closed. A small swatch of black mourning cloth hung from the doorknob. Affey, the Green Maiden, knocked exactly twice, as was the rule. Professor O'Riley bid them enter. His voice was sorrowful. It was not the booming baritone they were used to hearing.

He stood up when they walked in.

"I hear you brought back the Headmaster with a concussion."

Minda said, "news travels fast." Her voice too was soft and sorrowful.

"I'm afraid I have some bad news." The professor invited Affey, and Minda to sit as his conference table as they had done so many times before.

"We know, Professor," Affey said. "Kevin is no longer with us."

"I'm very sorry, Green Maiden. I know you held a special place in your heart for him."

Affey fought back her tears. "I did, I do, professor. It's hard to imagine Clonfert House without him."

"Green Maiden, I am afraid I have some other difficult news to share with you."

Affey, the Green Maiden, already knew what Professor O'Riley was going to say, but she couldn't bring herself to say it. "I know, professor, I know."

"What are you talking about Affey," Minda asked through her tears.

"The Green Maiden has passed while you were gone." Professor O'Riley sat down wearily in his chair. His sadness overcame him. He began to weep. Master Chan Wu entered through the library door at the back of the professor's study.

"Master Chan Wu. What are you doing here?" Affey asked quite surprised at his arrival.

He placed the sapphire staff on the table. "Kevin wanted you to have this."

She looked at the Master with eyes imploring him to explain. Master Chan Wu described the events at the Sorcerer Corradhu's private encampment. He finished by saying, "Mister O'Connell was more heroic than any of us could have imagined. If there is anyone who put in motion the Sorcerer Corradhu's, demise it was him. We will enroll him in the Book of Heroes. He will be enshrined in the Hall of The Masters."

Affey, walked over to one of the amber windows through which sun light poured into the professor's study. She stood there for a long time recalling every moment she spent with Kevin. She remembered his comforting words when she was so unsure of herself in the early days. Mostly, she remembered his kind heart. The others sat silently, respecting her time apart from them. She wiped the tears from her eyes. It was time to plan the funerals. She had no idea who was responsible for the arrangements or what, exactly, those arrangements were supposed to be. She didn't care. This was her friend, Kevin. She had lost her other dear friend, the seventh green Maiden.

"We must arrange for the funerals; Kevin's and the Green Maiden's. They will both take place here, together, in Saint Brendan's Cathedral. Professor O'Riley, will you please make the arrangements for Kevin. I will do the same for the Green Maiden."

"Yes, Green Maiden. What day shall we honor them?"

Master Chan Wu spoke up. "May I suggest two days from today? It marks the 500th anniversary of the Green Maiden's birth. We will have to close the cathedral without drawing attention. And you, Green Maiden, will need time to call for the former Green Maidens and Spirit Sisters to come as is the custom. The Oracle of the Dar Lantern must also come. She will explain what you must do as a part of the ritual. I doubt that the Green Maiden had time to tell you."

"She didn't, Master Chan Wu. I will send for the Oracle immediately. I am sure the former Green Maiden's and Spirit Sisters already know and are on their way here. Before we all leave, I have a question. Where are the Sisters of the Coven? I expected them to come to the sorcerer Corradhu's aid."

"Then you have some more news for you, Green Maiden," the professor said. "Major Lisset and her warriors captured only one of the witches and brought her here. She is imprisoned. The rest resisted. They were all put to death."

"Tragedy makes way for triumph," Affey said recalling the words of the prophecy.

Master Chan Wu asked, "Green Maiden, what of the Sorcerer Corradhu? Did he suffer the same fate as the Sisters of the Coven?"

"He was mortally wounded. I am sure of it. When he flew off into the sky, he dropped trails of blood behind him. I didn't go after him because I had to take care of the Headmaster and my sister. I have no doubt he perished shortly thereafter." Master Chan Wu and Professor O'Riley exchanged a doubtful glance. They wish Affey had gone after him to make sure he was dead.

Professor O'Riley stood up and went to his desk. He withdrew a small leather volume from his desk drawer.

"Take this with you, Green Maiden. It sets forth the ritual for Kevin's funeral. I have another copy. You should, know what to expect." Affey, the Green Maiden, took the small book from the professor and held it to her chest.

"Come, Minda. You can help me with the Green Maiden's funeral arrangements." She and Minda left the professor's study. Professor O'Riley and Master Chan Wu went to consult the Headmaster about Kevin's funeral.

The morning of the funerals for Kevin and the Green Maiden was as beautiful a morning as one could hope for. It was a bright, sunny morning. The flowers in the cathedral garden were bursting with color and fragrance. The world of Clonfert House was ready to bid Kevin and the Green Maiden farewell.

The Clonfert House choir began the ritual chants as the cathedral doors were opened.

All of the students of Clonfert House entered first. Gianni Giannotti led them in. His left wrist was bandaged. His right arm in a sling. He limped slightly. The students filled in the back half of the cathedral leaving the front portion for the professors and dignitaries who would attend. They were all dressed in their crimson scholar's robes. For many of the students, it was the first time they wore them. The crimson robes were only worn on those rare occasions when something extraordinary was to take place. The funeral of a student was one of the rarest of occasions. Gianni took a seat up near the altar. Once they were seated, the dignitaries arrived.

Each of the four quarters of the spirit realms sent a contingent of fairies, elves, nymphs, sprites, brownies, knockers, gnomes, ogres, and the like. They too were dressed in the most splendid attire. Because of the seriousness of the occasion, they all walked in. None flew or materialized from thin air. The kelpies arrived in a specially designed water globe.

Major Lisset and her female warrior spirits marched silently down the center aisle to the front so the cathedral. They were attired in their finest battle dress. Their shields were polished, the jewels on the hilt of their swords and daggers dazzled. The formed two columns down the sides of the center aisle from the foot of the cathedral altar all the way back to the cathedral doors. The stood facing each other.

Next to arrive was the faculty and staff. They were led in by the Headmaster, who was confined to a wheelchair accompanied by Professor O'Riley and Master Chan Wu. They were followed by Professors Mbaye, Smiley, Cornakova, and Howenstein, all of whom had mentored Kevin at one time or another. The last to enter and take their places were Kevin's parents, his brothers and sisters, and his uncle, Finnean O'Connell, the Clonfert China Regent who returned for Kevin's funeral. Once they were all seated, the choir began the Chant of the Soul's Migration. This signaled for Kevin's funeral procession to begin. Everyone, human and sprit, stood and turned toward the center aisle.

Major Lisset and her female spirit warriors snapped to attention. They drew their swords to form an arc under which Kevin would be carried.

Kevin's funeral procession was led by two senior students who carried a dark red banner with Kevin's name, birth date, and date of death embroidered on it in silver. It was made by a team of spirits representing each of the four realms. Directly behind them, six students carried Kevin's burial vault. The lid of the vault was inlaid with a mosaic of Kevin laying on his back. He was dressed in crimson scholar's robes. A likeness of the sapphire staff laid across his chest. He would be placed inside it as part of the rituals. Then, it would be carried to the Hall of the Masters, where he would inspire generations of students to come. The vault was carried to the foot of the altar where the students reverently placed it on the floor. The lid was slid off to the side.

The choir stopped chanting. A lone trumpet sounded from just outside the cathedral doors. Kevin's body was about the be brought in.

The trumpet sounded one, final, sad note. Then Kevin was carried in silently.

His body was on a special wagon. It was made of rough timber and covered with a blanket of raw wool. Kevin was laid out in crimson scholar's robe. His hands folded on his chest. He was at peace. The cart was drawn by six of the guardians of the Sacred Fairy Scrolls. They had never appeared to anyone other than the librarian before. They did it as a special favor to Michael.

Michael walked on one of the side wagons while Minda walked on the other. Walking solemnly behind them was Affey, her green radiance spilling over the wagon and Kevin. They made their way slowly to the cathedral altar. Minda, Michael, and the guardians took seats alongside Gianni. Affey stood silently for several minutes touching Kevin's folded hands. Then she ascended the pulpit. Major Lisset's women stood down.

"For those of you who don't me, I am the new Green Maiden. Some of you knew me at one time as Affey Temne, Minda's twin sister." A loud gasp rose from the students at the back of the cathedral.

"Today we lay to rest a real hero. Today I lay to rest one of my best friends. Kevin was brought here together with Michael, my twin sister, and me to help defeat Adena. You all know the story. Kevin was brave then. He was even braver two days ago. I want you all to know that Kevin gave his life so that our spirit brothers and sisters would survive. It is the legacy of this house. It is the legacy of our ancestors. Kevin, my friend, lived that legacy to its fullest measure. We all hope to find his courage when we are called to honor it ourselves."

"Today we stand together, spirit and human, only because my friend Kevin stands in the long line of sacrifices necessary to keep the world in balance. There is no way to thank him enough for what he did. The best we can do, the best we must do, is never forget him or what he did."

"We must also pause to honor those who fought and survived. Major Lisset, we honor you and your women. The Sorcerer Corradhu would not have been defeated without your actions. We must also honor my sister, Minda Temne, whose extraordinary power of Remote Viewing made it easier for me to face the sorcerer. Lastly, we must honor Gianni Giannotti. Most of you don't know that he is a master swordsman, a fearless and courageous fighter, and one of the kindest men I know."

"To you, Headmaster, Professor O'Riley, and Master Chan Wu, what can I say? You are the bastions of this house. We are all of us, spirit, and human, are forever in your debt."

"Clonfert Hose is a bulwark against the forces that would tilt the world out of balance. All of you assembled here today to honor my friend, your colleague, Master Kevin O'Connell, must renew your commitment to each other and to the wind and the woods."

The choir began to chant again. Affey, the Green Maiden, stepped down from the pulpit. She led Kevin's family to the wagon where they said goodbye to him.

The guardians of the Sacred Fairy Scrolls surround Kevin's body. They levitated him and placed Kevin softly in the vault. The lid silently closed. Kevin's mother could be heard crying. Six of Major Lisette's women picked up Kevin's burial vault and carried it reverently to the Hall of the Masters. Once they were gone, a crash of cymbals rang out through the cathedral. Trumpets blared. A slow steady drumbeat came from outside the doors of the cathedral.

The Headmaster tried to turn around in his wheelchair. Professor O'Riley and Master Chan Wu stood up quickly. Something was wrong. The former Green Maidens and Spirit Sisters were supposed to bring in the Green Maiden's body next. They were supposed to enter silently.

"Please, everyone be calm." Affey, the Green Maiden, gestured that the professor and the master should sit back down. The Headmaster, his voice hoarse, and barely audible, asked Affey, the Green Maiden, "what is happening?"

"You will see, Headmaster."

She lifted her voice and said to the assembly, "We have special visitors." Everyone turned in their seats toward the cathedral doors.

Drums beat steadily. Cymbals crashed rhythmically. Their combined sound drew closer and closer to the doors. A banner unfurled just inside the entrance to the cathedral. Across the banner were runes which read, 'The Twenty-Two Celestial Sirens'.

The sirens, led by the drums and cymbals, floated down the center aisle of the cathedral, their purple robes barely touching the floor. Their auburn braids strung with diamonds and emeralds. The cathedral was stunned into silence. Not one being in the cathedral, spirit, or human, had ever seen the Twenty-Two Celestial Sirens, except for Affey, the Green Maiden, of course.

Behind them were the Spirit Sisters dressed in their respective colors. The six former Green Maidens carried the body of the seventh Green Maiden. Her body was frail. Her emerald robe as now an earthy brown. Her skin was the palest green. Her hair was white as snow. They placed her body on the cathedral altar. Then, they stepped back to stand together with the Spirit Sisters. The Twenty-Two Celestial Sirens encircled the altar. No one watching them moved. It was as if the air itself stood still.

Affey, the Green Maiden, who had been standing off to the side was approached by two of the sirens who led her inside the circle. They had her stand close to the Green Maiden's body. The circle of sirens opened to provide a view of the altar so those assembled in the cathedral could witness what came next. One of the sirens stepped down from behind the altar to address them.

"I am the keeper of the prophecy that foretold all you have before you today. The death of one Master O'Connell, the passing of the seventh Green Maiden, the rise of her successor, the first mortal born Green Maiden. The prophecy foretold it all. The prophecy also foretold of the Sorcerer Corradhu. Our attendance here today brings that prophecy to a close. This is a momentous day. A day that will forever be remembered throughout all our realms. It is of such importance that we have come to escort the seventh Green Maiden to her next life with her Green Maiden sisters. Note our presence in your history books. You will not see us in this realm again unless you fail to learn the lessons from these events. Spirits, you too must record these events. We do not wish to return to warn you again. We will if we must, but we hope you will abide our warning. We wish all realms peace."

She returned to the circle of sirens at the altar. It closed around the seventh Green Maiden's body.

The drums began a slow, quiet beat. The lone trumpet sounded a haunting note from beyond the cathedral doors. The Twenty-Once Celestial Sirens began a chant that was so quiet the those assembled leaned forward in the pews to try to hear it. It was unlike anything they had ever heard, The notes seemed to move through them. The sirens started to sway. They raised their arms creating a rainbow that arched over the altar. The seventh Green Maiden's body rose from the altar. The former Green Maidens likewise rose from where they stood to gather in the air around their sister's body. The Spirit Sisters rose next to them. They turned slowly in the air beneath the rainbow. They carried the seventh Green Maiden's higher and higher above the circle of sirens. Suddenly, the cymbals crashed. A blinding light filled the cathedral blinding all inside. The cathedral went silent. So silent, that not a single breath could be heard. Then Affey, the Green Maiden spoke.

"Your sight is restored."

Every eye, no longer blinded, looked up toward the altar. There Affey, the eighth Green Maiden stood. She was accompanied by Botsam and the other guardians of the Eo Mugna Tree. She radiated rays of emerald light.

"I must return to the Eo Mugna Tree. We are all safe now. I am always at your service. I will watch over everyone. To my friends in the spirit world, we shall see each other often. Headmaster, Professor O'Riley, Master Chan Wu, but think my name and I will come. Michael, befriend my sister as she will be friend you. Your future lies here at Clonfert House, my dear twin sister. You and I will meet more often than you think. You will come to stay with me from time to time. We have so much to look forward to."

"I must leave you for now. The wind and the woods are balanced once again. As the prophecy foretold, 'all worlds orbit as one'." Another flash of blinding light filled Saint Brendan's Cathedral. The eighth Green Maiden, Affey Temne, was gone.

Epilogue

Peace reigned over all the realms for many, many years.

Affey, the eighth Green Maiden, with the help and guidance of Botsam and the other guardians, mastered all the Green Maiden's powers. Since the defeat of the Sorcerer Corradhu, she had not been called upon to intervene in any dispute, spirit, or human. She and Minda visited together often. Affey, the Green Maiden, was able to make short visits to Clonfert House.

Over the decades Clonfert House changed. Minda completed all her required studies ahead of schedule. She became Dean of the Department of Remote Viewing. She held professorships in Physics, Astronomy, and Thought Projection. She frequently lectured at the lower academies. Students sought out her advice. Her classes had long wait lists.

Gianni Giannotti succeeded the Headmaster when he died. Gianni took his responsibilities seriously. Too seriously, it turns out. Eventually, he succumbed to the rigors of being Headmaster. Minda was chosen as his successor.

Michael became the librarian just a few short years after the events surrounding the Sorcerer Corradhu. Professor O'Riley had an undetected heart condition that struck one day when he was alone in the Secret Library. Despite all of Master Bromley's efforts, he could not save the professor. At first, Michael refused the position. The Headmaster insisted he accept. Michael did so, but only after Master Bromley agreed to teach him everything Professor O'Riley was not able finish. Once he was comfortable in taking his place in Professor O'Riley's study and residence, Michael grew into the job. He and Minda befriended each other. They were as close as brother and sister.

Affey, the eighth Green Maiden, always made time to see Michael when she visited Minda. Michael always politely turned down her invitations to visit her at the Eo Mugna Tree.

Clonfert House settled into the rhythm of centuries old scholarship. The lower academies continued in accordance with the Clonfert Compact.

The fairy realms prospered. At Affey, the eighth Green Maiden's suggestion, the Sidda Council that governed the spirit realms, asked Major Lisset to lead the Western Quarter. At first, she refused. It took a visit from the Oracle of the Dar Lantern to finally convince her to accept. It didn't take long for her to restore order and prosperity to the realm.

All in all, the decades following the defeat of the Sorcerer Corradhu were some of the most harmonious ever experienced.

If there was one thing all this harmony and prosperity ignored, it was resolving what happened to the Sorcerer Corradhu. Their ignorance would cost them one day. The Sorcerer Corradhu survived. He wanted revenge.

Printed in the USA
CPSIA information can be obtained
at www.ICGtesting.com
LVHW011002020823
753722LV00007B/149